LV

MAY 3, 2016

D0016686

HEART ATTACK WATCH

BY THE SAME AUTHOR

God is an Astronaut

HEART ATTACK WATCH

Stories

ALYSON FOSTER

3 1336 09799 2524

BLOOMSBURY

NEW YORK · LONDON · OXFORD · NEW DELHI · SYDNEY

Bloomsbury USA
An imprint of Bloomsbury Publishing Plc

1385 Broadway   50 Bedford Square
New York   London
NY 10018   WC1B 3DP
USA   UK

www.bloomsbury.com

BLOOMSBURY and the Diana logo are trademarks of Bloomsbury Publishing Plc

First published 2016

© Alyson Foster, 2016

All rights reserved. No part of this publication may be reproduced or transmitted
in any form or by any means, electronic or mechanical, including photocopying,
recording, or any information storage or retrieval system, without prior
permission in writing from the publishers.

No responsibility for loss caused to any individual or organization acting on or
refraining from action as a result of the material in this publication can be
accepted by Bloomsbury or the author.

Portions of this manuscript have appeared in the following publications,
in slightly different form: "The Theory of Clouds" in the *Iowa Review*;
"Heart Attack Watch" in *Glimmer Train*;
"The Place of the Holy" in the *Kenyon Review*; and "The Art of Falling" in *Ascent*.

ISBN: HB: 978-1-62040-543-7
          ePub: 978-1-62040-545-1

LIBRARY OF CONGRESS CATALOGING-IN-PUBLICATION DATA:

Foster, Alyson, author.
Heart attack watch : stories / Alyson Foster.
New York : Bloomsbury USA, 2016.
LCCN 2015036441 | ISBN 9781620405437 (hardcover : acid-free paper)
|BISAC: FICTION / Short Stories (single author).
LCC PS3606.O7495 A6 2016 |DDC 813/.6—dc23
LC record available at http://lccn.loc.gov/2015036441

2 4 6 8 10 9 7 5 3 1

Typeset by RefineCatch Limited, Bungay, Suffolk
Printed and bound in the U.S.A. by Berryville Graphics, Berryville, Virginia

To find out more about our authors and books visit www.bloomsbury.com.
Here you will find extracts, author interviews, details of forthcoming
events and the option to sign up for our newsletters.

Bloomsbury books may be purchased for business or promotional use.
For information on bulk purchases please contact Macmillan Corporate
and Premium Sales Department at specialmarkets@macmillan.com.

To my parents,
Barbara and Stephen

CONTENTS

THE THEORY OF CLOUDS

IN SEPTEMBER, SCIENTISTS CAME to town to study the clouds. No one is sure how many researchers there are exactly—an undetermined number of men and a single woman who walks with quick and competent strides—and no one wants them there. The cashier at the gas station on Route 27 rings up the interlopers' purchases sourly, taking their proffered bills with two pinched fingers and grudgingly doling out their change, shorting them a quarter or dime whenever she can. The waitresses who serve them at the diner downtown leave their plates on the cook's counter until the mashed potatoes congeal and shun the tips they leave behind, making them fair game for the busboys who are untroubled by scruples.

Little surprise, then, Julia thinks, that the small group rarely ventures from their site at the southern perimeter of town just downwind of the plant. Every day, when she drives the school bus past the field where they work, she sees two or three of the scientists wading through the wet cresting grass, legs sheathed to the knee in bright galoshes, to where the spires of their instruments glitter. Or conferring over wide scrolls of graph paper that wave with hieroglyphics in the wind. Or draping themselves across the dented hoods of their Volvos, eating a sandwich with one hand and gesticulating skyward with the other. Their gestures are so earnest, so fraught with exclusive meaning that Julia looks up too, leaning forward in her seat to peer through the expansive windshield in front of her, as if something brief but majestic might appear.

She sees nothing. Her neck hurts, though. The hours of sitting, guiding the bus through the same rotation, twice in the morning, once at noon, twice at night—always right on Deerfield, left on Bluegrass, then left on Meridian, and then the whole pattern reversed—are tightening her joints like the cogs in a clock, everything forever grinding in the same direction. The fleshy undersides of her palms, that constant point of contact with the wheel, began to lose feeling several years ago, and now the skin there has a slightly deadened cast to it. She can see it in good light, faint smudges that never disappear, a bruising from wrist to pinkie finger.

She has never mentioned this to Danae; it doesn't occur to her. When Julia was a little girl, her mother used to call her stoic in an admiring tone. Now that her mother is gone, Julia likes remembering the word, the chime of it both melodic and steely in her ear. Another thing she keeps to herself. Danae has always thought Julia a touch sentimental. Danae, who works forty hours a week on the line at the plant sorting out the hardware that comes rolling off the belt. Her hands are as attuned to nuance as a blind woman's. Plow bolts from flanges, truss screws from pans, half-inch washers from three-quarters—Danae knows these distinctions by touch. Her fingers assess quicker than thought—all day long they sift out what they need and leave the rest behind. A metallic odor lingers on Danae's skin no matter how long she dallies in the shower. When Julia presses her lips to it the cold scent makes her think of snow.

Julia is out in the garden planting bulbs when Danae comes home late from the plant again. Three times this month, Smithson employees have been held after work for informational meetings. Julia isn't sure what information is being disseminated exactly. Danae can never quite seem to specify. But from what Julia can piece together these assemblies have an interesting tone—discussions that are strident and yet vague in their objectives. She patiently whittles out hollows in the dirt with her finger while Danae relates the most recent highlights. The summer flush of flowers has peaked and wilted away and now only a few hardy chrysanthemums remain, a spattering of stolid yellow and orange that glow in the gathering dusk.

"Are you listening?" Danae says, and when Julia looks up Danae repeats herself. "Joe Flynn was saying how we have to be careful," she concludes. "You know how these environmentalists are."

"Not really." Julia smoothes the soil with both hands and sits back on her haunches. The irises are tucked away now, ready for the cold and the waiting. She likes to sing a little song to her flowers while she lays them to rest for the winter, something to fortify them while the earth chills and hardens around them, but she would never let Danae catch her at it. "I mean I know how Joe Flynn thinks they are. But just because rabidity happens to be his natural state doesn't mean he should assume everyone else—"

"Rabidity." Danae shoves her hands in her pockets and tilts her head. "Is that even really a word?" She sees Julia opening her mouth and hastily continues. "I know it's a *word* word. But something people actually say? It isn't."

"Not Joe Flynn, anyway."

"Or anyone else." Danae reaches down and ruffles Julia's hair, traces the switchback of her part. "I get out in the world, Julia. I see things. One of us has to pay attention, even if you don't think it's important."

"Well, I'm glad you're up to the task." Julia stiffly hazards a standing position; dirt drizzles around her fraying tennis shoes. "I'm certainly not." Without thinking, she glances up. Too dark to see anything now—all she can make out is the pines' pitch and sway against a shadowy expanse. Beyond that everything is lost to the eye. Maybe the bats setting out above them or the birds returning to rest can still make something out, a glimmer of the clouds' churning passage, but how would anyone know?

"Hey." Danae gently scuffs Julia's foot with her own. "What are you looking at?"

Julia sees plenty. If you were to draw a map of her routes, they would spread out for miles in a series of intricate loops, widening like a net unfurling and coming back into itself. She drives the bus along gravel roads nearly hidden in the undergrowth. Three, maybe four times a year the county sends men through in giant threshing machines—they beat the weeds into shimmering clouds of pollen. Two weeks and the foliage has crept back up the shoulders and covered them over again. In some places oaks soldier up so close to the dirt tracks that the bus scrapes along their branches. The trees release their acorns like revenge. Hundreds drum down on the roof in peals of aluminum thunder before they scatter to the ground, each one to become a tree or nothing at all.

Julia no longer remembers many particulars from her high school education. But there is a vague concept from science class about time, how it's a dimension, like space. A dimension that can't be seen, only moved through. She thinks about this sometimes and wishes she understood it better. As the seasons pass, Julia travels along her convoluted orbit and watches the world change daily, hourly. Stones rising and sinking in the river beneath the bridge. Wildflowers blooming incrementally. A mailbox succumbing to rot and ditches filling with earth. An abandoned house accruing stars in its dark windowpanes, each one shining with its own crystalline light. Every year the kids coming back taller and more reluctant. While always in the distance the plant's three smokestacks jut like rust-tinged peninsulas into the sky. The smoke rising from them twists like musculature—a dense bunching that swells and darkens as it gains altitude.

In her mind's eye, Julia tries to merge this vast collection of moments, as if she could hold them all simultaneously.

She can almost picture it, the fields layered with every color there is, a frozen streak of train along the horizon, Julia herself coming and going, and the scientists suspended like ghosts watching the clouds hurtle through the sky, luminous mountains moving at the speed of light.

And then she snaps to again. Coming back into town, the bus passes the field where the scientists are working. The woman striding through the grass on the far end of it loses her grip on a sheaf of papers, and the wind takes them. In her rearview mirror, the inverted figure stoops and chases the sheets as if trying to call back a startled flock of birds. While the kids in the back turn to jeer.

Most days she's back at the garage by a quarter to four. The day is then her own. From there she often drives her Honda to the town's library. It's a one-room brick building with green carpeting, its ivy pattern nearly scuffed away by years of passing feet. Julia walks along the quiet rows as lightly as possible, imagining that she can draw up the creaking of the floorboards inside herself and leave behind nothing but silence. She closes her eyes, trails her fingers along the softening spines of the hardcover volumes, the splintering paperbacks. And then she stops. If the book beneath her hand isn't one she has read, she pulls it. If it is, she closes her eyes and moves on.

She rarely takes a seat at the table next to the sighing radiator in the corner. There's something vaguely depressing about watching the late-afternoon sun sink in the window covered in faded construction-paper stars from story hours long ago forgotten. She checks out her books from the word-less librarian and heads back out into the evening with the small stack of them clutched to her chest.

When she arrives home the paper is waiting, nestled in the top branches of the enormous jade plant on the porch next to the front door, placed there for her by Danae when she leaves the house each morning. It's a shabby little local publication, never more than fifteen pages long, and the photographs are poorly set, the red and yellow ink misaligned so that every figure trails behind a forlorn blue ghost of himself.

The reporting isn't so bad, though. Tim Kelley, the *Herald*'s editor, has a reputation for being eccentric. The property where the scientists are now at work belongs to him; he's letting them camp out there for free. But Kelley also has family that goes back generations in the town; he's related by blood or marriage to school board members, plant foremen, and town councilmen, and is therefore a known element. His loyalties cannot be called into question, and besides there is nothing else for them to read.

Julia reads the paper every day from first to final page. She's not especially interested in the particulars of any one story—the conflagration of a granary out on North 46 or the deranged high school band director fired at last with great fanfare. It's more habit than anything else, following the dramatic arcs of business and personal tensions like plots in a mediocre sitcom, predictable but still moderately diverting.

And then even the humdrum offers up a revelation from time to time. When Julia opens the paper one fall afternoon she finds a letter to the editor on page two written by one Christopher Tenley, leader of the enemy conclave, the authoritative addendum to his surname: Ph.D., Atmospheric Science, Cornell University. Who around here can compete with that? She puts the water on to boil, shakes out the paper, and sits down at the kitchen table to read.

That's where she's sitting when Danae comes home. The water has boiled away and evaporated into nothingness, and not until the thump and shuffle of heavy shoes on the linoleum does Julia smell the empty pot, a metallic scorching in the air. Danae appears before her in the haze, jacket in one hand, her face wrinkled up wryly. "Smells great," she says. "Hope you saved some for me." With her free hand she gestures toward the paper. "What do people have their panties in a twist about now?" she says. She herself never reads a word of it.

"The usual, lately." Julia sits up and rubs her elbow, which has gone numb. "They think the EPA is going to come in here and close us down, and we'll all be jobless and starve, and the children will turn feral and run naked through the streets."

"Oh yeah?" says Danae. The second syllable bows a little under some kind of extra thought she's not saying, but Julia has jumped up to rescue the pot, to keep the bottom of it from adhering permanently to the burner, and so she doesn't notice.

"You should read it, Danae," she calls into the living room. It's too late—the burner has singed a scar of concentric rings into the pan's copper underside, and the entire kitchen is rife with a poisonous stench. "Kelley printed this whole long piece by the guy that's heading up the study. Tenley is his name. He's trying to explain what it is they're looking at. He says there have been some studies about certain airborne industrial emissions—that there might be something in them affecting atmospheric patterns. They think the plant is actually making new clouds. How crazy is that?"

The window above the kitchen sink won't open—it has been carelessly painted into its sill. Julia's handiwork. Danae would never have done something so shoddy. Julia leverages all the power of her pitiful biceps for one last push, and finally it gives in a burst of white flakes.

"They just want to know, that's all, Tenley says," she continues when she catches her breath. "I mean, it could have important environmental consequences. But of course Kelley put this guy's letter—which is very dispassionate and well-written—next to these accusations that people like Flynn wrote in. And he didn't edit out any of their typos. He just put *sic* in brackets next to all their mistakes. Then over the top he put a big headline that says, Whom do you believe?"

No answer. Still waving her hands at the smoke, Julia steps through the doorway to see Danae standing by the table, frowning down at the paper. Finally, she looks up. She's been rubbing her short brown hair against the grain, and now it bristles up like an animal pelt. She says, "Kelley better be careful."

"Oh, come on." Julia starts to laugh, and then she sees

Danae's scuffed knuckles tighten against the seams of her corduroy pant legs.

"No, you *come on*, Julia." Danae picks up the paper and begins twisting it into a funnel, wringing it tighter and tighter until her fingertips blur the newsprint and come away dark. "I know you think bad grammar is funny, but this isn't a joke. These are people's jobs—it's *my* job."

"Don't you think it's possible you're getting just a tad ahead of yourself?" Julia puts her hand on the back of a chair to steady herself. The room sways, just slightly, around her ears, but she's startled at how ready she feels for a fight, pitched forward on her toes in a battle stance. "No one's talking about shutting anything down, Danae. It's *science*. Widening the scope and depth of human understanding so we can better our situation. So they find out it's true. It doesn't mean they're going to *do* anything about it. But the thought of facing a few unpleasant facts—"

"Blah, blah, blah." Danae folds her hand, fingers to thumb and snaps them open and closed in Julia's face. "Facts, my ass. You're the one who reads the paper. They went up to that electric plant in Grayling just to do a study. They sent people out on that forest property owned by the Hyatt Mill just to do a study. They went out and took samples of phosphate or whatever the hell it is up in the Titabawassee *just to do a study*. And what happened afterward in those places? Not nothing. Kelley may think he's being smart, and you might get a kick out of it, but he's not doing anyone around here any favors. And neither are you."

And with that pronouncement she whirls, a single tight and

enraged pirouette, and marches out of the house. A moment later the truck engine throbs to life, but Julia can't hear it. She's still rocked back on her heels, dumbfounded, ears ringing.

Overnight the wind swings around to the north. It scrapes abrasively across the woods and fields, the benign remnant of summer suddenly sucked out and gone in the night. Danae appears in bed next to Julia sometime early in the morning, and she doesn't stir when Julia cautiously loosens the blankets from around her hips and leans over her. Danae's boyish face with its square jaw is still fierce even in sleep, her fists tucked under her chin. Neither one of them is old exactly, but in bad light like this, the embalming gray tints before dawn, Julia sees the future. Her own flesh has already begun to separate out: tendons, muscles, and veins all coming slowly toward the surface. It is now apparent that Danae will be one of those old women chiseled down into sinews by the passing years while Julia will simply go soft.

In cold weather the bus drivers arrive at the lot a few minutes early to warm up the buses before they start their routes. They wave at one another, beat their gloved hands together, and lean their backs against the bright yellow hulls, talking and drinking coffee out of Styrofoam cups. Julia can't abide small talk, especially not early in the morning. She slips past them with as cursory a nod as she can manage. As soon as she pulls the bus door behind her, the conversation resumes. While she waits for the mammoth engine to warm, she paces up and down the center aisle. Cold air bristles around the bus's twenty-two windowpanes—she pinches the catches on several of them and slams them closed, but they only settle back down in their frames again. Well, we'll live, she thinks. She pulls a broken pencil out of the fold of the front seat. Gold butterscotch wrappers gleam on the dusty floor and absentmindedly she bends to pick them up. She watches them crinkle and spark in the palm of her gloved hand.

It takes a long time for the air in the bus to lose its edge even with the heaters on at full blast. Paisley and peacock-feather patterns of frost recede from the metal frames and then from around the messages that the kids traced in the condensation during the last cold day. Most of this childish cuneiform is cryptic to Julia's eyes, but there are the obvious tic-tac-toe games and the initials wedded together—*VN + EW*, *AF + DB*—in valentine hearts. The order, always the lover first and then the beloved, Julia does remember. She isn't sure how these inscriptions vanish and reemerge—and she's thinking about the physics of it, the memory of glass, when the sun at last clears the trees, and burns the elusive letters into silver decrees that make her eyes smart and sting.

They continue to run all morning, not tears exactly, just a steady filling and emptying. The bus's mirrors concentrate the immense pallor of the sky from all its angles and funnel them into blinding pinpoints that slip into her pupils and inside of her. Clouds are running like liquid through the afternoon sky, small rivulets flowing around denser deltas of gray, and only every now and then does she see a snatch of blue in the depth of their passing, an insinuation of something hidden and vast.

How crazy is that? Her own stupid question reverberates in her head, as she turns the bus north onto Bluegrass, west on Whiteville, south onto Meridian. *How crazy is that?* A crumpled doe lies just on the shoulder at Hiawatha and Lantern Hill, casualty of the blind left curve. For days Julia has watched the animal's disintegration; now its white ribs are slowly unfurling like stark pinions on the verge of flight. *How crazy is that?* Whatever word she should have said last night to Danae about Tenley's letter, it wasn't *crazy*, that trite adjective. Granted, every other word she might have chosen also sounds childishly overstated when uttered out loud, but still.

She's wandered so far into the thicket of her own thoughts that the intermittent chatter of the other drivers over the radio and the sound of twenty-seven children rampaging in a rattling hothouse of breath and motion is utterly lost upon her, but when the wheel trembles under her fingers Julia starts straight in her seat, guilty, as if she'd spoken aloud without being aware. She jerks her eyes to the road in front of her and then glances up in the trembling mirror that hangs over her head. None of the kids seem to notice. Several factions in the backseats are kicking at one another from across the aisle, behavior Julia has forbidden. All her rules are unenforceable and ignored.

They're losing speed now, continuing to slow no matter how hard she depresses the sturdy gas pedal beneath her foot. The bus sways with increasing gentleness over every rut; the yellow lane dividers stretch out longer and longer with their deceleration.

"Why are we stopping?" calls a voice from behind her. "We're not at Blake's house yet." Julia doesn't turn around. She keeps her foot to the floor. For one insane moment she believes she has driven them all into a surreal inverted world, and the trick to keeping them going involves letting off the accelerator bit by bit.

Then she returns to her senses. They are at a dead stand-still in the middle of the road, five miles from the elementary school, not far from where Tenley and Co. have set up camp. Behind her, the kids surge up in their seats, each one straining to see something amazing before his neighbor does and thus gain an authority no one else can share. An ominous reek begins to filter in through the vents.

"If the bus is broken do we get to go home?" asks the voice. Julia thinks she knows whom it belongs to, but she doesn't look back.

"No, you do not." She fumbles with the radio next to her. Normally she listens to the call-and-response banter of the other drivers with a secret annoyance and no intention of ever joining in. She presses down the button on the mouth-piece with her thumb. "Hey," she says and apologetically identifies herself. "This is 89-A here. We're having some mechanical difficulties, and I don't think we're going to be able to make it in." A silence ensues; for a full minute she believes no one will answer her back.

Even though she'd told them to stay in their seats, the bus erupts into riot the moment she steps off and pushes the door carefully almost, but not quite, closed. Julia can feel the vehicle rocking slightly with the impact of footsteps pounding up and down the aisle while she struggles to lift the bus's yellow hood. The garage's last refresher training session on engine maintenance and emergency repair was years ago, and once Julia manages to release the cover over the engine—it opens backward, the hinge over the head-lights—and locate the prop to hold it up—she has done everything she knows how to do. Black smoke pours off the massive engine block, which now gapes in the open air. Julia stands on her tiptoes and ventures to peer down into it, but the choking cloud drives her instantly back. She doubles over, coughing into the grass, sucking in the windy cold and waiting for her lungs to clear.

When she straightens again, she sees a figure moving toward her from the far end of the field. A few more seconds, and it resolves itself into a man; he's moving, head down, without haste, and from a distance she thinks he's lost in some ponderous thought. But no, as he draws closer, it becomes clear that he's kicking an aluminum can in front of him with each step, somehow driving it upward and clear of the weeds, without ever losing it or syncopating his stride. His hands are shoved in his pockets, and he is, astonishingly, wearing nothing heavier than a sweatshirt.

He lets the can fall to rest when he comes within speaking distance of her but pauses before he says anything. His mild eyes survey the scene; his hands knuckle around in his pockets as if searching for an elusive piece of change. Julia waits, somehow struck by the notion that he should speak first. It's still early yet—there's no sign of anyone else, only a single vehicle parked far on the other side of the field, and so this, she believes, must be Christopher Tenley, Ph.D., in the flesh. The shrieking of the children vibrates in the space between them, high-pitched trills that pass straight through the windowpanes as if they are as insubstantial as air.

"So the mutiny was successful," Tenley says at last. "Is this the island they've voted to leave you on?"

Julia turns and looks back. All of the faces have disappeared behind filmy curtains of condensation—the only things visible are pink segments of fingers that creep like earthworms over the glass. "They can't leave," she says. "I took the keys."

"Smart woman." He hitches the neck of his sweatshirt over his nose and steps up to look down into the engine.

"Don't bother," Julia says. Suddenly she's at loose ends; having two arms seems superfluous. She crosses them across her chest and rubs furiously at the coat covering her shoulders. "There's nothing to see."

He doesn't seem to hear her. "Really, it's okay," she says. "I already called it in. They're sending the mechanic. And another bus. We just have to wait."

"That could be it." He steps back and pulls the shirt from his face. The smoke has dissipated although the engine continues to bake the air, making the backdrop of fence posts and red-gold trees wobble like flames. "There's some sort of belt giving out—down near the back. Look, you can see it."

"Really," Julia says, but he has her by the sleeve and guides her alongside of him. "I won't be able to—"

"Right there. Near the carburetor. Maybe it's not the carburetor. I actually have no idea. The construction of this engine is bizarre."

Julia follows the line of his finger, through the blackened assortment of greased shapes, and then she sees it—the fraying of something silver, a cluster of needle-fine spines.

"There it is. I see it." She means to pull back, but instead she wavers uncertainly, staring down at the glinting thread-bare ends. The warmth of the engine wafts up across her cheeks. Hedged in by Tenley and the bus, she is now shielded from the cold teeth of the morning. The wind acts as a current streaming his heat into her and carrying it away again. He stretches out his hands, rubs them together, camp-fire style over the engine block, and after a moment, she follows suit. They stand there together, propped on their elbows, staring down into the bewildering jumble of parts and wires, listening to the soft hissing sound of them fading gradually toward silence. She says, "I read your letter."

Tenley doesn't look up. "Ah, yes. The letter. Apparently, it wasn't such a hit." He reaches out and brushes the studded half circle around the bus's wheel well. "Someone keyed my car."

"Oh." Julia does not know what else to say.

"Hostile locals. I don't remember them covering that in grad school." He's still tracing the raised trail of yellow rivets with his fingertips, already pursuing some other thought. "Are these Smithsons?"

She glances down and laughs, a single flat syllable. "Are you kidding?" she says. "Of course they're Smithsons. The county specifically ordered the buses from a factory that uses them. Most of the buildings around here are held together with Smithsons. My house included. The realtor made a point of mentioning it to my roommate. Did you not see the sign on the way into town?"

"I saw it," he says. A car approaches; it must be Frank, the mechanic, coming grudgingly to the rescue at last.

"So you think it's true?"

"What? The theory about the clouds?" Tenley scratches the back of his neck, and they both straighten up, take a step back into the cold. "I don't know. There are still a lot of other things to rule out. But you want my gut feeling? Based on the data we've seen so far, yes. It's true."

"So then what?"

Frank is bearing down on them now in his rattling hulk of a tow truck. Julia can see his face, the scowl of disapproval growing more distinct with each passing second.

"Then what nothing." Tenley gives a little wave toward Frank as the truck slows and settles heavily into the soft shoulder just in front of them, a gesture Frank clearly does not appreciate and does not return. "That's not my department. I just study clouds. Clouds are amazing. I want to keep learning everything I can about them until the day I die."

Julia means to tell Danae about the encounter. She really does. It's once she starts thinking about the logistics of the telling, how to begin, where to leave off—that she comprehends the difficulty of it. She keeps shifting around the pieces of the anecdote, and still something is just not right. When Danae comes through the door that night, she is whistling between her teeth, a thin and determinedly cheerful melody that marks the end of every workweek. It signals her intent to let bygones be bygones—*bygones be begonias* is what the two of them say—and as soon as she hears it, Julia knows she will not say a word. It is the sound of the moment passing her by.

Friday evening is their dinner out. They cycle through four of the town's five sit-down restaurants, passing up the fifth, a pseudo-Chinese establishment, because every dish contains water chestnuts, which Danae will not tolerate. Tonight it's Stuckey's, a steel-and-glass-plated greasy spoon that serves only breakfast food. It is the only place open all night, and therefore it draws the drunks and the lonely, but at this hour it is perfectly respectable. The diners pass by the tables saying hello to one another, inquiring after the health of one another's folks, spouses, and children. A couple of Smithson men sitting near the corners wave a hail-fellow-well-met to Danae as the waitress leads them to their booth.

When their food arrives Danae attacks her tangled nest of bacon. She always eats like this, as if each meal is a serious duty that must be dispatched without delay. Her small body burns through its fuel with a disconcerting inefficiency. It's as though the strain of never quite being sated has keyed it to a febrile pitch, giving her coloring an almost painterly quality—copper filaments in the ends of her hair, a flush touching her cheekbones and clavicle where the indigo collar of her stretched-out sweater hangs even beneath the muted glow of the chandelier between them. Julia picks at her food and watches the taut working of Danae's jaw. It's up to her to carry the conversations at the beginning of the meal; Danae will pick up the slack at the end while she waits for Julia to finish.

She scrapes at the purple sauce covering her pancakes, searching for an actual blueberry, and talks on about the garden, which is being plundered by the deer. They've been exceptionally bad this fall, laying waste to everything including the chrysanthemums. Deer are supposed to be repelled by mums, but these deer are not. They bring their family and friends to the feast, and they devour her flowers down to nubs. The topic strikes Julia as safe. She does not want to break this truce, the normalcy still brittle around its edges. She can feel it, the way she is trying a little too hard.

"Oh, the mums," Danae says between bites. "You know what you should do. They sell coyote urine over at the garden store. You sprinkle it on your garden, and it keeps them away. I can get you some if you want."

"No thanks." Julia has discovered a berry at last, albeit a shriveled one, and she spears it triumphantly with her fork. "I don't like this idea of buying pee to soak my garden. If I'm going that route, why don't I just save the money and piss on it myself?"

"That would probably work." Oblivious Danae doesn't look up from her plate, and instantly Julia's heart leaps out toward her, that unshakable and endearing practicality. She forgets herself and reaches out across the tabletop to squeeze Danae's free hand. A momentary lapse. Julia has broken their cardinal rule—*never where other people can see*—and immediately she pulls back, but not before Danae's fingers elude her grasp, withdrawing from the scalloped border of the paper placemat and into the depths of her lap. It is not the first time Danae has reminded her. The reproof never quite loses its sting, a sharp dwindling feeling that amplifies every sound around her—the clatter of the plates, the scraping of chairs—into painful twinges in her ears.

When Julia's eyes clear, they are focused somewhere in the background, and it's then that she sees Tenley. He's sitting across the aisle three rows behind Danae, and Julia can't understand how she hasn't noticed him before. Maybe because the hostess has seated him in the back, at a darkened table beneath a burned-out chandelier. Maybe because his head is bent over—Julia can just glimpse them around the curved red lip of the booth—an elaborate fan of papers. He has anchored them down to the table with flatware, but the edges ruffle up in the breeze of waitresses swinging in and out of the kitchen doors.

"I'm going to run to the bathroom," Danae says. The table tilts unsteadily as she pushes off and then disappears.

Julia is not sure where to look. She's trapped beneath the chandelier's swaying hoop of light and blushing conspicuously for no good reason. Where is their check? She thinks she sees it in the waitress's hand, but the girl is dallying by the hostess' stand, leaning over it and swinging her rump thoughtlessly from side to side as she talks. The sway of her skirt's pink folds against the back of her thighs has caused the table of Smithson men to put down their forks. All Julia needs to do is wait out the next few minutes, pay the bill, and get away. These are not difficult tasks. She turns and studies her reflection in the blackened window beside her. The sharp twisting this unnatural posture requires, the effort of narrowing herself into a mere sliver of a profile hurts her shoulders. But she holds it with great determination, stares at the blanched moon of her face floating in the glass. Then something stirs and ripples the image.

"You made it off the island, I see."

Julia turns and glances up at Tenley. Then back over her shoulder. There is no sign of Danae. Perhaps she has been waylaid by a table of colleagues and has not yet found her way back. "I did," she says. "It was a hard swim."

"I'm glad." The restaurant is overheated to the point of suffocating, but he's still wearing that navy sweatshirt with the sleeves pushed up. He might be exothermic and simply prefer to warm and cool with the air around him. Even in the bleached light his forearms look tan. It's not the thin veneer sported by vacationers—it's the weathered coppery cast of someone who works under the sun during even the harshest of days. The coarse hairs covering them shine. Julia can't bring herself to lift her eyes any higher.

"So look at what came out of my table." He opens his hand and drops a screw among the cutlery in front of her. Julia watches it revolve in two slow circles before it settles to a stop. "You know, I'm not sure about these things. They seem prone to stripping out. The radii of the turns might be too short. That's my theory."

Julia rocks in her seat and anxiously jiggles her legs up and down as if she's running in place. "I wouldn't know anything about that."

"Well, nothing to lose sleep over." Tenley squats and props his elbows on the tabletop, and Julia lifts her head and looks him squarely in the face for the first time that day. He's smiling at her, but he stops abruptly when she meets his eyes. Their irises are richly detailed, a patchwork of blues embroidered with intricate white stitching. The sudden serious straightening of his mouth makes her stomach drop in a sickening way. From somewhere across the restaurant, Julia hears Danae laugh, her stage laugh. It's half an octave high and a beat too long.

"All right, then. I'm on my way out of here." Tenley quickly straightens to his feet. "I just have to browbeat that waitress into taking my blood money. Given how little they're probably paid here, they should get a pass on principle, don't you think?" He lays his hand against her back, a brief pressure, there then gone. "Take care, Julia."

"Take care," she mutters.

Half a minute later, Danae is back, flushed and triumphant. "I just heard the greatest story," she says. "Wait until I tell you."

But Julia doesn't hear a thing. She's too distracted by the gaze of the burgundy-haired woman sitting in the booth behind them. Julia recognizes her—a teller who works at the bank across town. She is staring at Julia with the hawkish and satisfied expression of someone who has just had her least charitable suspicion confirmed. There's something so steely, so chilling in its import that Julia falters and stumbles mid-stride.

The Smithson men turn to watch them pass.

"Ah, home to bed." Back in the passenger seat of Julia's car, Danae flings out her arms—embracing the warmth streaming from the dashboard vents, the night, the happy lazy weekend ahead. She slithers out of her seat belt and rests her head on Julia's shoulder. "You're beautiful, Julia. Have I told you you're beautiful?"

"Of course you have." Julia's tone is sharper than she intends. Beneath the thick layer of her jacket, the imprint of Tenley's fingers still lingers on her nerve endings, a five-point brand seared across the rise of her left shoulder blade. This confounds her: she can't for the life of her remember telling him her name.

"Well, I like to say it." Danae shifts dreamily. Her mouth finds the chink of space above Julia's collar and nestles gently against the bare skin there. For the rest of the ride home she stays like that, so still she's barely breathing. Julia can feel the carnal press of Danae's pulse beating through her dry lips, slowing only when she finally drops off while Julia's races on. Clouds have covered the moon; the night is so black that the headlights cannot possibly keep up with their speed. Every turn, every curve of the road holds the split-second possibility of peril.

On Sunday, just back from their trip to the supermarket, it befalls them. Danae sees it first. Julia is doubled over the seat of the hatchback, wrestling a tangled bag of groceries, which is resisting her for all it is worth. When she hears the sharp intake of Danae's breath, she drops it and stumbles out ungracefully, ass-first into the bright day.

"Jesus Christ," Danae says.

There is the jade plant, scattered. There are the dismembered branches, the spread-eagle stems, each one twisted from its joint so savagely that pale green viscera gapes from each severed end and gleams wetly in the shade of the porch. There are the pot's blue shards, still quivering separately like blades. There is the strewn dirt. There are the thick oval leaves, dozens of them, loosed and flattened. All of this Julia sees, but so startling is the effect that she cannot reach backward through it to grasp for a cause. Everything inside of her has hardened and become as brittle as glass, and so she simply stands and looks and listens to the wind seethe in the dry autumn grass.

Danae is racing up the steps, throwing back wild speculations about the wind, about deer and their ability to climb stairs—suggestions so ludicrous that Julia would laugh if her mouth weren't so dry.

"Julia."

Julia has regained the power of motion once again. She stumps up the walk like someone on peg legs, climbs the stairs, peers over Danae's shoulder, and together they stare at their front door. Centered in the green paint a single word has been etched, DYKES, all in capital letters. The lettering is rough and its lines are deep and deliberate. They have been carved by a heavy hand through the layers of the door's history—freshly exposed shades of red, blue, yellow, and gray curled out for all to see—and straight into the grain of the wood.

"Someone *did* this." Danae sounds amazed. She says it again.

Julia's first thought is to get inside as quickly as possible. The outdoors seems full of open, dangerous space; the sky yaws with it. The inky ellipses on the cluster of birches at the far end of the garden leer at them like eyes, and all she wants is to get her back against a corner, the thicker and more opaque the better. The lightning hit of adrenaline shot along her nerve endings has begun to fade, and although her knees still tremble she manages to pull Danae through the door and slam it shut behind them.

Once inside, Julia jogs from window to window, lowering the blinds. Danae stands adrift in the foyer where Julia released her. She keeps scuffing her hair, dropping her arms, then reaching up and scuffing it again as if concentration alone will produce an answer to this new and perplexing question. "After all this time," she says. "Why now?"

The blinds have cracks between them. Their curtains aren't much, just gauzy strips filmed over at the edges with dust, but Julia pulls them for good measure. Danae vaguely watches the flurry of activity, still adrift. "I just don't understand," she says. That's what she keeps coming back to. "I just don't understand."

By the time Julia goes out to the car to retrieve the groceries, the ice cream has melted and spread. When she opens the hatchback, a marbled puddle spills over the bumper and drips across her shoes, and the entire car smells sweetly overripe like berries.

The day wears on. Julia can't sit still so she gets down on her knees and begins scrubbing the floors. The fierce repetition of her arm across the rippling linoleum soothes her—the moment it stops she feels the dread again, a swift renewal that stops her breath every time. Bucket after bucket of water muddies and turns black.

Danae keeps wandering by the window and peering between the blinds. "I just don't understand," she says. She stares out into the dusk. "I just want to know why, that's all, you know?" She lets the plastic slat snap back into place, but she can't restrain herself; she peels it up and looks again. "After all these years. You keep your head down. You toe the line. You do your part. And this is how they felt all along. That's the worst part of it."

"For God's sake, Danae." She flings down the sponge. "Hasn't it occurred to you it might just be some kids? Don't you remember being in school? Kids just *do* things. Why do you have to attach all this significance to it? Maybe it doesn't *mean* anything. Maybe it's just stupid."

But when Danae turns from the window, Julia can see her eyes shining. "I know," Danae says. "That's what I keep thinking." She angrily brushes her face with her sleeve. "But something is off, Julia. It just doesn't feel right. It's like the sound of something turning on you. Can't you hear it?"

Julia picks up her sponge and wrings it dry. Very formally she says, "Please put those blinds back down."

Everything seems significant now. On Monday morning several children on her route are absent. Julia reminds herself that cold season is beginning. There are those weeks when some plague or other cuts a swath through the public school system. This could be one, although it seems early. Normally she makes it a rule not to wait at her stops, but today she idles at the end of empty driveways. A few of the teenagers glance up at her as they board the bus, maybe gauging her, maybe not. They are always a shifty-looking bunch, unwilling to let on how much they know. Or don't.

All day long, the radio is quiet. Every quarter hour or so, Julia reaches over and changes the frequency, trying to catch someone somewhere else, but there is nothing but the empty rustle of static, quiet stirring air.

Lunchtime, back at the garage. When Julia pulls her brown bag out of the refrigerator, she catches sight of a red slash mark on the calendar over the day. Someone has written her name above it, first and last, in exaggerated scrawl instead of the usual initials used for notations. The high school cross-country meet in Chesaning at five o'clock tonight. Somehow, she's now on the schedule for the extra shift. When she sees it, Julia feels her peripheral vision fading to black. So here it is. She rips the sheet from its tacks and marches into Henry's office.

He's sitting in his desk chair, feet propped on a dented filing cabinet, playing a game of Solitaire on the garage's ten-year-old computer and doesn't look up when she shoves the door open. "What can I help you with, Julia?" he says. The hulking monitor is dying; he has to lean in to make out the faces on the cards.

"What." She thrusts the paper toward him. "Is this?"

He doesn't turn his head. "That would be the overtime schedule." He clicks twice on the mouse and leans in closer to peer at the dusky screen. "Is there a problem?"

"Why am I on here for tonight?"

"Marlene has a doctor's appointment. She needs to leave early."

"What about Rob? Or Erin? Or Carl?"

"You were up."

Julia's hands are shaking so hard she can hear the paper rustling. She drops her arm to her side and tries to speak as levelly as possible. "There are at least four people in the rotation ahead of me. There is no possible way it can be my turn."

"I checked. It is."

Another click. Stacks of cards flicker away. One of the arms on the chair is coming loose. Julia watches it tilt back and forth beneath his elbow. She says, "This is bullshit."

"Excuse me?" At last he turns to look at her. Henry has been around for ages. He's seventy-six weeks away from retirement and his pension. Every Monday morning he calls out the countdown to whoever happens to be in the garage. This might be the longest conversation the two of them have ever had. His wide face is impassive as a slab, and he wheezes slowly in and out for a few seconds, waiting for her, before he continues. "I have a copy of your contract in a file right over there, Julia. Mandatory overtime requirements are spelled out on page three if you want to have a look." He slides his feet off the cabinet and lets them fall heavily to the floor. "It also states that you're an at-will employee. You're clear on what that means, right?"

Through the window, the fleet of buses is parked in lines. It's strange to see those identical bright shapes layered in rows, like a stuttering of the eye. Julia's gaze wanders across them, the matching black letters and stripes, the emergency back doors, each one manufactured in precisely the same dimensions. Once a year the drivers are required to have a drill in which the children unlatch them and leap out over the rear bumper into the grass. Even for an adult, Julia thinks, it's a long way to the ground.

Without saying another word, she turns and leaves the office. She slaps the crumpled paper back up on the bulletin board, stabs a single pin straight through the center of it, and goes to use the phone.

Danae eats lunch every day with a group of men from Smithson. They get half an hour between the bells—the one releasing them and the one calling them back—never quite enough time to come home, so the employees who don't bring their lunches pile into cars together and race out for hamburgers and French fries wrapped in greasy paper sheaths. Danae is small enough to squeeze into someone's lap—that's what she told Julia, pleased with the image of herself—her head pressed up against the ceiling, someone else steadying her feet.

Julia intends to leave her a message on the house phone, to tell her that she will not be home until eight o'clock at the earliest. She dials the number and tears furiously at a loosening seam on the cuff of her jacket while she waits through the rings, ripping out the loops of broken stitching. When someone picks up after the third one, she is so startled that she nearly drops the phone. The hello on the other end sounds like a stranger's—low and ragged—someone Julia has never spoken to in her life, and there's a lag before her ear registers the pitches. All the hair stands along the back of her neck. *Danae*, she says, *Danae, it's Julia.*

A long and tremulous pause follows. Julia listens to Danae breathing, the way each exhalation sounds like a struggle to keep something in or to hold it at bay. The scouring sound of each one against the receiver is deafening. Julia reaches out, places her hand against the cool cinder block wall beside her and closes her eyes. Something is coming back to her, a night, years ago, back in the days when she and Danae were still new, and every moment together seemed profound in some way. It had been spring, and the smell of lilacs sifted in through the darkness of their open bedroom window. They had been talking—of what?—until Danae drifted off with her head on Julia's chest. While Julia breathed in and out beneath the weight of it. At last, she couldn't bear it anymore. *Danae*, she had whispered, shifting out from under as gently as she could. And Danae, not asleep at all, had lifted her head in the darkness. *It sounds like a storm in there*, she said. The husky catch in her voice had startled Julia into silence.

"Danae, listen to me." Julia can feel the tiny openings of the phone's mouthpiece like perforations in her own skin—she's holding it that hard against her face. She knows what she means to say: *It isn't like that. It isn't what they told you.*

But when she opens her mouth what comes out is, "I'm sorry." The line goes quiet, and Julia immediately calls again, but this time no one answers.

The afternoon stretches out, an infinitude of space and quiet. The sky above them a taut blue plain. Julia can't remember the last time she's seen it so clear. There's something aching about its emptiness. With nothing in it the expanse seems depthless—nothing can be discerned of all the distance it contains or the speed of those shifting currents of air passing soundlessly overhead. Julia feels weightless, disembodied, as if everything—the sounds of the children talking, the golden trees burning along the fringe of the horizon, the steady mechanical vibrations of the bus engine—must travel a long way to reach her. And by the time they have, they are simply faint impressions of what they once were. The wheel spins frictionless beneath her hands; the bus takes its corners in loose and fluid curves. Julia moves with great care—one thoughtless gesture, one emphatic twist of her shoulders and she could send them all hurtling down an incline, or straight through a guardrail into the river. It would be so easy to do. She sits straight and rigid in her seat, studies the edges of the road crumbling away, mile after mile, in glittering obsidian chunks.

When she finishes dropping off the last of the elementary school kids and pulls up in front of the high school, the cross-country team is waiting for her, a swarm of leggy kids in gold singlets and faded blue shorts. They storm the bus as soon as she opens the door, loaded down with their cleats and coolers. There is a charge they carry with them of low-grade anticipation. The race is ahead, waiting to be run. The girls work their hair through its bands, shake it loose, collect it again, and every one of them talks too loud.

On the way out of town, they pass the field where the scientists are working. The boys in the middle seats are hurling bottles full of jewel-colored liquid—aquamarine, topaz, and sapphire—back and forth across the aisle, deaf to the coach's admonitions, while the girls discuss the difficulty of taking a piss discreetly in the woods. Julia wills herself not to look, but she sees Tenley anyway for the first time that day. He is standing alone in the field, a lean silhouette, staring skyward. Far above him a lone cirrus wisp hangs like a plume, something lovely he has single-handedly concocted from the blue. When he hears them coming he turns his face. He lifts his hand and salutes her as they pass while Julia stares straight ahead, eyes burning, and pretends not to see. One of the bottles goes flying out the window, splits on the asphalt, and its bright drops scatter like ruby light receding in her rearview mirror.

It's a relief to finally reach their destination, to be able to stop and let the landscape, which has been rattling past, come to a rest at last. Julia opens the door, and everyone flows out and away, and then she shuts the door tightly behind them. The driver in the bus next to her, a balding man, has slumped against his driver's side window and covered his eyes with his hat.

But Julia can't doze. She can't read. She hasn't even thought to bring a book. She stares out the windshield at the sun slanting over the gutters of the empty school building, the shining empty troughs beneath the sky. *There are billions of water droplets in a single square foot of cloud.* That is what Tenley's letter had said. *The weight of them all added together numbers in the hundreds of tons.* Julia has no idea what keeps them in a holding pattern overhead. She drops her head to rest on the steering wheel in front of her and studies the patina of her fingerprints across the plastic, slick spots, still visible in the fading light. The days are getting shorter. From the parking lot, she hears the sound of the starter's gun, and when the runners come back to the bus, their limbs are like ghosts', glowing blue-white with the chill in the air. They smell like sweat and fallen leaves. She can't remember what happened to that letter now—if Danae took the paper out the door with her that night as she left, or if Julia herself placed it in the stack to be put out at the curb, anxious to be rid of it. She wishes she could recall more of it now, just a few more words, but they are gone, and no matter how long she thinks back, there is nothing else.

By the time they make it back to town, it is dark. The plant is always the first thing you see at night, a complicated web of interlocking lights, red and golden cells in an ornately gridded backdrop. They infuse the sky with a dingy peach hue, reduce the low-lying buildings in the foreground to nothing more than two-dimensional outlines. Julia has studied the vista more times than she can count, driving this bus with load after load of students, year in and year out. There's something about the final stretch, when they have passed beneath the last of the monolithic bridges and left the last curve of the interstate behind them, when the highway looms emptily like a straightaway before them— acute fatigue sets in, as if all the miles she has driven thus far are nothing compared to these unbearable few she must complete. This is what is referred to, Danae once told her, as losing your sense of proportion.

But when has knowing such a thing ever helped? Right at this moment—as Julia grits her teeth and bears down on the accelerator, determined not to slow down, determined to hold them all to their course, to return them to where they came from without shirking or delay—she can't put aside the thought that it all looks terrible in a way she has never noticed before. *Inferno* is the word she keeps thinking— something about the way the horizon flickers, dark and lurid at the same time—and then she realizes it's the smell that's unsettling her. Something is burning.

It's been quiet in the bus, but behind her a stirring begins, a steady swelling of voices, and now everyone is sitting up, alert, straining to see the road ahead where they are bearing down on it now—to where the asphalt shines out in an unearthly streak of light. The dark landscape ebbs around them, flickering shadows, straight lines warping into curves, but off to their right through the next stand of trees, they can see it at last. The field is ablaze. The dry grass roils with flames; the wind has carried its sparks up into oaks—their branches are alight, unfurling. Gusts of incandescent leaves whirl through the air, showering down upon the expanse of fragile wildflower skeletons, all ignited, each one black and vivid.

The coach has come up to the front of the bus. Julia does not know how he got there. He is speaking to her urgently, yelling perhaps—it's impossible to hear anything above the raging air outside her window and everyone around her pantomiming frantically—flashing hands and wild faces like signals in a language she is unable to comprehend. She hasn't so much stopped as taken her foot off the accelerator. She depresses the parking brake; when she stands and pushes open the door, the metal is alive to the touch.

As loud as it was inside the bus, it's so much louder out here, as if the sky is sundering. She drifts a few steps off the shoulder of the road, stops short where the ground drops into a dry drainage ditch. The heat is blistering, radiant and painful across her throat and lips and fingers. Somewhere in the distance, glass instruments burst and shatter in ringing octaves.

Julia listens to the sound of them and watches a cluster of figures emerge from out of the smoke. They walk with quick and steady strides, their hooded heads unbowed, hands swinging gasoline tins, metal tinged black, their emptied sway light and triumphant. Seven or eight or twenty of them, forms like apparitions, but Julia recognizes only one.

The squared shoulders, the fierce strides matching the others' step for step. "Danae," Julia yells out. "Danae." And when Danae turns back, when she lifts her eyes defiantly to meet Julia's they are so bright with the fire that Julia doesn't call out again. The sound of the conflagration has begun to dim around her until the world is simply rising and falling in the profoundest of silence, and everything it contains—the flames, the smoke, the lights and shadows, the unraveling fence, the lamenting birds taking flight—is simply acquiescing gracefully to some force she can just now perceive, some pattern of air or eddy of the sky. She can only raise her eyes and watch the dark billows surge up into the air, collecting over the burnished trees and disappearing into the night above them.

HEART ATTACK WATCH

THE BACK OF THE sublet that Maggie and I moved into after our sophomore year faced a road favored by ambulances. Two, sometimes three times a night the siren-scream pitch of someone else's calamity wailed me from sleep. The walls of my bedroom flashed rapid pulses of red before disappearing back into refreshed darkness. Then I lay awake and waited for my heart to slow down again. On the other side of the wall, Maggie, in the throes of another philosophical crisis, paced lengthwise along the boards of the hardwood floor. In the sudden dearth of noise her steps were distinct; each creak bent around the perpendicular angle of the wall and raced like a rat all the way to the ceiling over my bed. Once I noticed these irregular fragments of sound, I could hear nothing else and not even the din of crickets or the shushing noise of traffic could silence them.

There were lots of other things wrong with the apartment. Water seeped from the base of the kitchen faucet.

Loosening nails made evenly spaced blisters in the ceiling plaster. The linoleum in the kitchen curled up at the corners. When it rained, the silverware drawer wouldn't open. If you dropped a pen on the floor it rolled southeast every time. Two days after we moved in, the bathroom door caved off its hinges. When one of us wanted to take a shower, we lifted the door and propped it across the frame in an approximation of covering. As we rubbed shampoo through our hair, we ignored the drafts that fluttered the shower curtain and the black constellations of mildew flecks spreading above our heads.

Maggie, Margaret, Marguerite, Marguerita—that was how Henry shifted along the variations of Maggie's name and the more beers he drank, the more syllables there were, the more exaggerated the vowels. No matter how drunk he was when he said mine, it fell dead, like a rock into a lake: *Jane.* He fed the two of us dinner the first day we moved into the apartment above his. Maggie and I had thrown out everything perishable before we hurled the contents of our dorm room into sagging brown boxes and plastic bags. By the time we finished unloading, all the food we had between the two of us was a box of cornflakes too stale to crackle and a package of ramen last seen in a pile of Maggie's pilling sweaters and AWOL since then.

The forest-green door to our apartment, bearing fresh nicks from Maggie's ten-pound barbells, had gaped open, and Henry had knocked twice on the doorframe. He asked if anyone was there.

I looked up from the box I had just opened. I had hoped to discover a clean towel and some soap. Instead there was purple taffeta. Two summers ago, my mother—now 457 miles away—sent me off to college with the fervent belief that I would, at some point, attend a formal. Nothing I had said could convince her otherwise. The dress now had creases that would never iron out.

I wiped my grimy palms along the skirt's smooth folds and asked if I could help him.

The question, he replied, was whether or not he could help us. He lived downstairs and had seen us moving in. Did we need any help? His head jutted from his shoulders like a pitbull's.

No, I said. I always wanted to get rid of strangers as quickly as possible. I told him we had everything, but thanks.

Still he stood there, looking in, and not subtly either. His craggy face turned a full 180 degrees from one side of the apartment to another. He took in the cardboard-box mountain range stretching over the floor. The garish abstract prints framed on the walls above it. "I can feed you," he said.

Down on Henry's patio, Maggie and I stood around a rusting grill as the smell of beef wafted into the air. Henry squashed one patty after another onto a platter. Maggie was so hungry she ate three of them in a series of rapid bites, no ketchup, no buns. I turned my attention to the stack of American cheese and browning lettuce.

A black dog, steaming from the rays of the setting sun, loped across the lot from behind a scraggly row of bushes.

Her tongue spilled from her open mouth, and she watched the grill with reverent eyes. With one hand, Henry absent-mindedly brushed the heat out of the dog's fur, and he told us about how he'd been in the space program back in the 1980s. Just around the time the women astronauts were getting all the attention, he said. When he went to bring out a picture from inside his apartment, Maggie looked pointedly at me, but neither of us said a word because the sliding door was wide open.

We looked at the photograph, an enlarged 4x6, slightly out of focus and, sure enough, there he was with Sally Ride, or someone that could have been her, hair feathered into a dark brown lion's mane. Both she and Henry wore blue spacesuits, and they were looking off in opposite directions as if they didn't realize they were sharing the frame.

Henry had left Houston and NASA and come to this town because he'd fallen in love with a woman and thought life wasn't worth living without her, space or no space, moon or no moon. Now she was gone, and his pension wouldn't get him much more than the apartment, a matinee or two a month, and dog chow for Io. You would think that they would give more money to someone who used to orbit the Earth on a regular basis, but people generally aren't valued as much as they used to be.

Maggie, I saw, was entranced by this. Gone from her mind was Descartes, the evil deceiver, or the problem of free will. She lounged in a fraying lawn chair, arms resting on her stomach. Her bare legs, which hung out of running shorts, were dotted with the darkening preludes to bruises, a history of each cardboard corner and edge she'd struck since she'd gotten out of bed thirteen hours earlier. She soaked up every one of Henry's words so she could repeat this story later to someone else when she thought I wasn't listening, embroidering it with her own witticisms and elaborations.

Meanwhile, Io and I stared at each other. The dog's chin sank to the cement. Her eyelids came together, pulled apart, came together again. The consciousness guttered out of her gaze. She fell asleep. Darkness settled just at the edge of the patio. I could see my knees but not my feet. The world shrank to a slit between my own eyelids and expanded again.

Henry talked on to Maggie. Space smelled coppery, he said, like coppery burnt toast. You could smell it when the astronauts went in and out of the cabin door. Even after they closed it, the scent lingered around the edges, and sometimes he used to sniff around the seal for the leftover molecules.

Up and down my forearms, the mosquitoes feasted, touching down and lifting off again. And I was tired, dead tired, so I simply let them.

A week after our move, I started working the first shift as lifeguard at the rec center half a mile away from our apartment. Early Bird Swim was its official title, but since only a few people who came between five thirty and nine o'clock were under sixty-five, the other guards referred to it as Heart Attack Watch. My high seat on the shellacked chair at the end of the walkway, between the rectangle of the lap lanes on my right and the square diving pool on my left, poised me perfectly to see both length and depth, but the water, always shifting slightly but always looking the same, gave me a headache.

It could have just been the chlorine in the air. Around me the walls peeled green flakes, the color of a wilting houseplant. The acoustics of the huge auditorium amplified the smallest sound, but by the time it reached the dusty rafters, skipped over the rows of empty seats, and came back to your ear, it was so blurred that it was unrecognizable.

A whiteboard at the end of the lap pool was scrawled over with a down-slanting list of rules left by the water-safety class instructor. Each night she erased the top of the board and wrote a new quote, which Martina, the guard who relieved me at nine to do the toddler swim, called the "Cliché of the Day." *Don't frown*, it said, *because you never know who might be falling in love with your smile.* Or maybe, *Dance like no one's watching, love like you've never been hurt.* Martina read them aloud to me every morning. Then she flicked away a contemptuous imaginary tear. Two years ago, she'd almost made the women's Olympic swim team, but she just missed the final cut. Her body was built to stroke the butterfly with shoulders that looked as if they had been knocked out with a chisel.

Throughout my shift, intent old men and women in swim caps kicked and paddled slowly up and down the lanes. No one crossed the aisle to the diving pool except for one woman who came every morning and floated alone in the turquoise space. She lay facedown on the surface of the water, arms stretched loosely out from her sides. I watched her the most, and sometimes I counted. Every sixty to eighty seconds, she lifted her face for air. When I saw her take a breath, I inhaled.

Her name was Lydia Cohen. More than one swimmer who came to chat with me at the end of their laps informed me of this. Gerald Cohen, her husband, had passed six months ago, really a wonderful man, and did I know him? They thought it was a shame that I hadn't. Anyway, ever since his death Lydia had been coming in the mornings to float in the diving pool, and though no one quite understood what she was doing, they hoped I didn't have a problem with it, because sometimes people simply need their space.

It wasn't a problem, I said. During my conversations, I nodded, smiled, and gave the appropriate answers, but the whole time I was counting, the seconds running through my head like numbers on a stopwatch. *Fifty-two. Fifty-seven. Breathe.* By the time Martina showed up, Lydia Cohen was always long gone. No ripple in the water to show where she'd been.

By the time we'd been in the sublet about a month, we were eating dinner with Henry about once a week. He made fruit salad, every piece in it cut into a cube, and macaroni with chunks of ham that I painstakingly picked out. Maggie discreetly drank the cheap beer he offered out of a coffee mug, as if any of the neighbors would care. Fat flies thwacked against the screen door behind us.

Maggie asked Henry about going to the bathroom in

space. It was one of her more burning questions. Every night she thought up a different one and waited until she'd had a few beers to ask it, face flushed flirtatiously, feigning embarrassment. The details of personal hygiene in zero gravity fascinated her. I speared a square of strawberry with the crooked tines of my fork. Henry told us about vacuum-seal toilets. He told us that if you try to shave without cream, the stubble floats up and gets in your eyes. It was extremely important to chew with your mouth closed. Everything floats around in space; you have to always remember that. That's why they give you salt and pepper in liquid form, because otherwise the granules escape, and you can breathe them into your lungs while you're sleeping. Those were his tidbits for the evening.

"So I told you what I know," Henry said to Maggie. "You tell me now. Tell me what you know, Marguerite."

Maggie pretended to think hard. Then she said, "I know there's no free will." She'd spent four semesters trying to find someone who could convince her that this wasn't the case. But they couldn't. She'd gotten into a long discussion with one of her professors once, and he'd told her— She stopped, searching for the right words so that she could use quotations, but she wasn't able to find them. So she continued without them. He told her that philosophy was beautiful analysis, that it was a way to craft arguments, launch them, and see how well they flew. But he said if she was looking for meaning she should know right then that she wasn't going to find it there and to think hard about why she was doing it.

"Launch, schmaunch," Henry said. He waved his hand in the air. "Human beings may not have any free will, Marguerita, but we can send people into space, dammit."

"Exactly," Maggie said. "So fuck this philosophy bullshit." They laughed, and her elbow banged the table. Some of her beer slopped onto the dog, and they laughed even harder.

"Jane's not laughing," Henry said. Out of the corner of my eye, I could see him watching me. "Why don't you tell us what *you* know?"

"She's grumpy because she doesn't know much of anything these days," Maggie said.

I thought, I know you guys are assholes. I said nothing. Already the sky was turning black, and still it was so damn hot.

Back when I went away to college, people assured me that I would find something that interested me, that this was my time for joyful self-exploration. By the time I finished my second year, I knew these assurances for what they were: hopeful lies. The insidious truth revealed itself to me bit by bit. I carefully read the assigned books from start to finish. I diligently followed the lines of Locke's arguments, and Marx's proclamations, and Melville's plots as if knowing each word would save me, kick-start my sluggish brain, disprove what I dreaded might be true: there was nothing in me to explore. I thought of my internal space as a dry little plot with a gray sky overhead. You didn't even need to turn your head to see everything there was.

Sometimes during my sophomore year, wandering through

campus quads cut across slantwise by sidewalks, I would flicker my eyes through the tangles of bare tree branches. I would follow with my gaze the lines of mortar that wove around the bricks of the classroom buildings—up and out in every direction—possible to trace with your fingers if only you were tall enough, if only your arms could spread that far. And I would realize with panic *that I wasn't thinking any thoughts*. Think of something, think of anything, I told myself. And I couldn't.

I didn't speak of this to anyone. Only Maggie knew that at the end of the summer, she would start classes without me. The registration period for my junior year had opened and closed, and I simply let it pass. In June, my mother called to ask me why she'd never received a tuition bill. I told her that the family of the man who'd invented the pop-top had donated two million dollars to the university with the stipulation that it be used to fund one year of every undergraduate's tuition. My junior year was going to be free.

My mother expressed skepticism. Surely the newspapers would have run a story on it. People like that normally just want buildings named after them. Besides, she hadn't gotten any notification. Shouldn't the university have sent a letter? I said it was coming. The administration was still hashing out the details.

"Figures," she said. After another minute, we hung up. Maggie, sitting at the dining room table, looked up from the pages of *The Will to Believe*. "What are you going to do?" she asked. I shook my head, a side-to-side don't-ask motion, and she returned to her book without saying anything more.

One night in mid-July, I followed Maggie's lead and asked for a beer with my dinner. Once I managed to overlook the terrible bread-burp taste it left in my mouth, I found that I no longer cared about the heat. I slouched in my chair, sweating, the bottle resting on my chest in a single cold spot of relief, my thoughts no more lucid, but less ominous. Tufts of grass that had fought bravely up between the cracks in the slab made it to the baking air and then proceeded to die. I finished my beer and opened another.

In orbit, Henry said, you complete a rotation around the Earth in about forty-five minutes. The windows of the shuttle protrude a bit, so if he pressed himself up against the glass concavity, the walls of the cabin disappeared. He liked to feel as if he were alone in the cold, watching continents and oceans pass beneath him, rising up over a bright edge at the east and falling away into the darkness in the west.

"It is not possible to imagine," Henry said, but he went on describing anyway. He especially loved looking at the side of the world where it's nighttime. You could see the cities like nodes of light, dispersing into points and thinning out into threads bright, then faint, like webs across the blackness. When he stared hard, he believed he could see the major interstates, I-70, maybe I-75, but they wavered under his direct gaze, so he could only see them in his peripheral vision.

Sometimes he imagined all that light shining off into

space as a sound, Henry said. Like an orchestra warming up, just after the first clarinet player strikes a note, and everyone else joins in. A million different pitches converging into something beautifully layered and dense.

"It's impossible to imagine," he said again.

But I thought I did. Maybe that was why tears sprang to my eyes, although they did not spill over the lids. I lifted my thick tongue. "Is it lonely?"

Henry stopped talking. They both looked at me. "Is what lonely?"

"Being in space. Watching the earth revolve underneath you like that."

He lifted his beer and a few drops slipped from the bottle onto the bone-white concrete beneath him. "Yes," he said finally. "I was always looking, trying to orient myself because the world doesn't really ever look like it does on a map. The discrepancies throw you off. 'There's the Pacific,' I'd say to myself. 'That point jutting out must be India.' I thought I could see Denver right in the middle of the U.S., which is where I grew up, but I could never be sure. I'd figure out what time it was for them down there. I'd tell myself, 'Okay, they're probably eating breakfast right now.' Or that it was evening rush hour. And of course none of them were thinking about me. They had no idea I was passing by up there. I'd think of all the physics equations it was going to take to get me back here. There are only a handful of people in the world who can do them, you know."

"Now that's profound," Maggie said. I hadn't recognized the silence until her words bracketed its end.

I stood up unsteadily, alarmed by the way the ground listed away from me and the plastic chair glided off from my groping hand as if friction no longer existed. I had never been this drunk before. I said I had to get up early tomorrow morning.

"Jane, Jane," Henry said. "Come back to us, Jane. The night is young, Jane." I wove my way through his dark apartment and back into the hallway. The stairs tilted and loomed, and I climbed them with tremendous effort, one after another, one after another, one after another. *Eighteen. Nineteen. Breathe. Breathe.*

It rained the next morning. The drops blew in through my open window and wetted the bubbling paint on the sill. Each bleat of my alarm drove a spike into my temples. Humid air hung in my lungs, and a shiny plastic sweat clung to my body with nowhere to evaporate. Keeping my eyelids closed over my bulging eyeballs, I managed to wrestle into my swimsuit. No point in showering. I twisted my hair into a knot and stumbled out the door to find my dripping-wet bike.

I pedaled toward the rec center through the empty streets. No one was out yet; the windows in the tilting Victorian houses were still dark rectangles, life suspended somewhere behind them. On the high school track, four runners raced alongside one another. As I pulled up next to them, they rounded the curve of the homestretch, and I could see the sheets of rain bursting across their thighs, all four strides in sync, one perfect flash after another with every footfall.

I must have slowed down somewhere along the way because somehow I was late. The first few swimmers were politely waiting at the double doors outside the pool. I flicked on the lights, climbed wearily into the guard chair, and laid my heavy arms along the rests on either side of me. The men and women sorted themselves into lanes. Lydia Cohen climbed into the diving pool and began to drift. Her arms swayed with the rise and fall of the water, as if she were conducting a song she alone could hear.

I leaned back in the chair and let my head fall, stared up into the rafters, through the ceiling, up past the cloud cover, past where the sky was blue, up into where it went black. Henry had told us that astronauts were up there right now. Maybe they were passing over the rec center at this very second. I imagined for a moment that it was possible for them to see the lights of this town, the roof over this ceiling, that I was at least a blip on the radar screen if only that.

My eyes were closed, I realized, with a jolt. My body jerked and my heels smacked against the footrest of the chair. Was I forgetting something? I cast my gaze over the pools, at Lydia Cohen. Her neck looked limp. I straightened in my chair and stared. If I'd been counting, I would have known. Without my count, I was lost. Where was I? Forty? Seventy? Three hundred?

"Mrs. Cohen?" I called. There was no response. I leaped from the chair and slithered along the rungs, elbows and shoulder blades knocking the way down, but I landed on my feet and ran to the edge of the water. "Mrs. Cohen?" I knelt and slapped the surface of the water with the flat of my hand. She did not move except for a slight turning of her body with the wrinkle of the water's surface.

I dove in and two strokes brought me alongside her. I knew something was wrong the moment I placed my hand on her back. She was so still.

Although she was in the corner closest to the ladder, it took a long time to get her out of the water. I caught her under the arms and heaved her up onto the cement, the roughness of it snagging the skin on my knees and the tops of my feet. I swung her legs to the side so that she formed a parallel line between the two pools. Such precision seemed incredibly important. Everything had to be done just right. She lay there, a strangely large and awkward mass of dark blue nylon and wet skin that gleamed before my eyes.

I sought a heartbeat, resting my head against the slick fabric of her swimsuit, my cheek sinking into the giving flesh of her motionless chest. It was impossible, this absence of animation. I could distinguish nothing but the sound of my own blood, thundering furiously through my alarmed heart. Where were the smooth transitions that I had practiced in all my classes? Every second seemed severed from the one before, a flurry of disjointed movement—my thoughts coming in short bursts, stalling again and again.

I leaned over, lifted her chin with two fingers, and opened her jaw. It yielded easily, and just for one moment, I hesitated, my mouth hovering above hers. Her lips were dark purple, the shape of a distorted heart. I could see each line in them, tiny fissures giving way to the dark hole of her open throat. I closed my eyes and leaned down, covered the limpness of her mouth with my own, forced the contents of my lungs into hers with an unanswered urgency. Four exhalations.

I straightened, searching with my fingers along her sternum for the correct point where the bones and muscles met, the correct alignment that would give me the magical place, the hidden button to restart that still heart. I pounded on it, begging it, ordering it to respond, to recommence its simple exquisite cadence, before bending back to her again. It seemed inconceivable that she should fail me, that the sheer force of my will could summon no answer.

I don't know how long I went through the motions. CPR, in training, is a series of numbers. Two breaths should be followed by fifteen chest compressions at the rate of a hundred per minute. But the counts I wheezed out were a senseless jumble in my ears. The compressions I thumped on the unresponsive chest were paced at the rhythm of the pounding inside my own, the exhalations that I forced from myself, the hurried release of my own lungs.

I was bent over her mouth when she resumed living. I felt the clench of her airway, and the sudden vacuum rush in her windpipe, rising to take my offered breath. Her inhalation was so sharp that it pulled the last of the air out from the bottom of my chest cavity, and in that moment it seemed as if my own life was being sucked away. I recoiled, pulling my hand from where it rested on her forehead. Water spurted from the corners of her mouth in small streams, and I lifted my shaking fingers to wipe them gratefully away. She took my hand in hers, gripping it so hard for someone so old, so alone, someone just back from the brink. She wouldn't let go.

There was nothing left inside of me. I lay down next to her on the concrete, and waited for the paramedics. People stepped to my right, above my head, and below my feet. Far up in the rafters, the fluorescent lights bloomed, sending tiny rays out in every direction. They remained sharp and bright no matter how many times I blinked my eyes to clear them, and so I continued to stare, dazzled, as voices rose around me, and the siren of the ambulance wailed to life somewhere in the distance.

SAND CASTLES

THE FIRST MORNING WE arrived in Grand Marie, Jeff and I hiked with the girls along the bluffs to look at the disintegrating houses. We walked through the empty doorways, brushed sand off the sills, tore Queen Anne's lace from the foundations, and tucked the flowers behind our ears. Jeff stamped on the stair boards, then raced to the top to lean out the yawing bay window at the front of the master bedroom and smell the wind coming off Lake Superior. He mused aloud in lyrical phrases about waking up to the sunrises that burned across the expanse of the water, then fell silent as he rubbed the flat of his hand along the banisters. The seasons had worn away their dark finish and left each railing with a peculiar patina.

I stayed on the first floor while Patrice and Caitlin waddled around in the rectangles of light demarcated by the framework of studs and support beams. It was their first summer here and only their second summer in the world and therefore impossible for them to comprehend how much earth had fallen away since the last time we'd seen this place or know that somewhere—who knew where exactly—a developer had bitterly cut his losses. Erosion this breathtakingly swift could count as an act of God, like a storm or a stroke. Two steps off the porches brought you to the brink of the bluff. Even the long grasses and tenacious pines that leaned out into the empty space above the beach could not stay the crumbling. Every now and then, in the gap between the waves, the second before one rushed out and another crashed in, you could hear a clot of sand dropping from the clutch of a root and exploding on impact at the bottom.

Our own cottage sat safely away from the beach, and it took a five-minute trek through the sparse woods to reach the lake. The property lines were dubious; we trespassed unapologetically. After Jeff's grandfather died and left him the cottage, we'd come every summer except for the last one, after the twins were born. We weren't locals by any means since we turned tail and ran south back to Indiana when the first chill of September rolled in, but we'd transcended the tourist category to carve out our own niche. If our neighbors saw us in passing, they bobbed their heads in acknowledgment—the man with the waist-length beard and a feather stuck in his John Deere hat, the grizzled cashier who sold us produce at the town's only grocery store. These natives resembled the local foliage—tough and fibrous, carrying within them through the brief summers the knowledge of the dark freezing winters when life must hunker down and endure. I occasionally overheard their predictions. The boy who threw rocks at the Newmans' dog would grow up to steal cars. The teenager who stared at her reflection in every window she passed was turning into a slut for sure. What they said about Jeff and me—the poet and his freakishly tall wife—I could only imagine.

And now there were the girls, one dark, one fair, fraternal fairy-tale twins. Snow White and Rose Red, Jeff called them although I complained half-seriously about the connotations these words carried. A poet, of all people, should understand the weight of a name. The tangles of cause and effect could not be teased apart. But even at this young age the differences between my daughters struck me. Caitlin's sunny path stretched ahead of her: blond homecoming queen, diplomat, easy traveler through the world.

My own nickname for Patrice was Frowny. I didn't know babies were capable of looking so disgruntled. She brooded for a quarter of an hour on end thinking her own annoyed thoughts while Jeff and I studied her face and tried to determine whether she was going to have a single frown line in the center of her forehead like Jeff did, or one next to each eyebrow like me. It was difficult to tell; her smooth infant skin barely wrinkled no matter how hard she scowled. I suspected already that she was the child who would require our cajoling. Sometimes at night, when I checked on the girls, I leaned over and spoke into her ear, *It isn't that bad, Patrice.* I knew she didn't believe me. She sighed in her sleep and pushed away with both arms.

Maybe the flashing from the lighthouse disturbed her, like it did me. Despite the protection of the trees and the calico-scrap curtains drawn over the windows, rhythmic flashes bled through the darkness like lightning. When I couldn't sleep I stared at the knotholes covering the walls and ceiling. By daylight, they were intriguing dark whorls in the amber boards. But obscured by shadows, they became more ominous, hundreds of little vortexes all around us, the shape of them more nebulous. Mornings, when I went to wake the twins, I would find Patrice already awake and worrying over the black concentric rings with her gaze.

An all-day rain shower occasionally made captives of us and forced me to concoct quiet diversions for the girls while Jeff paced around the loft and tapped fitfully at the keys of his laptop. By the end of his sabbatical he wanted to have a completed collection of sonnets and an essay on formalism. I kicked around a beach ball and Patrice and Caitlin chased it over the undulating floorboards, gaining their sea legs. Or they fingerpainted cumulus shapes in red and purple—the only colors in our pitiful paint set—onto the scrap paper that bore Jeff's rejected stanzas. I hung the sheets on our lime-green refrigerator, a faithful hulk of an appliance, circa 1975, that would never give up the ghost.

For the most part, however, we passed the days and evenings out of doors where the rest of the color spectrum sparkled and shone in the sunlight. I took Caitlin's finger and pointed to each pristine shade. "Blue. Green. Yellow. White. Brown." Jeff plucked up Patrice's hand and poked at the gradations. "Cerulean, Patrice," he said. "Aquamarine. Navy. Saffron. Emerald. And don't forget gray. That's going to be an important one for you."

When I rolled my eyes, he defended himself, telling me that adjectives were important and he wanted his progeny to have as many avenues of self-expression open to them as possible. He loved so many words; he had a difficult time selecting the one he wanted. He conceded that all the choices bogged him down. But that's why he admired the stringency of the sonnet's form. It disciplined him, he said, forced him to drop away his descriptors one by one. A painstaking process, but it left something honed and sharp on the page. According to the critics anyway. He waggled his eyebrows at me. I sighed again, and he yanked up a stalk of puzzle grass by the roots and affectionately whipped it against the back of my thighs while the girls shrieked, and gulls scattered up from the water's edge.

On the third weekend in July, Grand Marie held the Sand Castle Competition and Sand Sculpture Exhibition. It was the town's sole claim to fame, and people came from all over both the lower and upper peninsulas of Michigan to compete for the five-thousand-dollar first prize. RVs crowded the town's single main street, and clusters of tents sprang up along the beach like nylon toadstools. The ice cream parlor stayed open until midnight, and the taps in the dingy pub ran almost nonstop. The air carried an odor of burnt sugar and beer that dissipated only in the early morning and collected again by noon.

I thought we should try our hand at a sand castle. Despite Jeff's disparaging remarks about Midwestern culture or the lack thereof, I convinced him to fork out the ten-dollar entry fee, and the four of us rose early on Saturday morning to make our way down to our assigned patch of sand, designated by marker number 163. The contest organizers dredged up an enormous amount of extra sand from somewhere farther down the beach and then rolled out piles of it along the watermark. Presumably this was to keep the castles clear of the lake's clutches until the next morning when the judging would take place.

Half an hour into the creative process, I gave up because the twins kept wandering away. Once they started moving, it was hard for them to stop, and I worried they would go crashing through someone's moat or demolish a turret. So I left Jeff to fend for himself and lured them down onto the packed sand at the shoreline. The frigid water turned their feet blue, but they didn't seem to notice or mind.

While the two of them flirted with the waves, I watched contestants attack and mold the sand with fierce concentration. Boys ran back and forth with buckets, men plied trowels, girls carved out elaborate curlicues with forks and sticks, and women patted damp bulges with their cupped hands, trying to smooth out any potential fissures, then reached up and patted them again. Adolescents fiddled with their swimsuits and pretended to be bored before they were harassed into participating.

It amazed me how fast the shapes rose up from the flat expanse of the beach. By noon some of the structures stood as high as my chest. It would have been possible for Caitlin and Patrice to walk through some of the archways if I had let them. The sculptures were no less impressive.

A western and eastern hemisphere bulged up from someone's plot, their geography detailed enough to include Sri
Lanka, Madagascar, and, of course, Michigan. Another
group attempted Michelangelo's *David*, but the right
shoulder had crumbled, and they were trying unsuccessfully
to salvage it. Two other people worked away at an enormous
hand. One of them hollowed out shallow trenches, bringing
tendons into relief, while the other etched out the puckers
over the thumb joint with a tire-pressure gauge. The skin on
their backs was burned bright red, but still they kept working.
Most likely, they just hadn't felt it yet.

I brought Jeff an overpriced hot dog for lunch. I don't
think he'd taken more than a five-minute break from his
castle since he'd started hours ago. Instead of block-by-
block construction, he opted for the sand-drip method.
He'd burrowed beneath the dry top layer of the beach to
extract the wet sand pooling below the surface, then meted
out the grainy brown liquid between his fingers in dribs
and drabs, adding and adding. With the foresight that
came so naturally to him he'd made the foundations of
his towers ample enough to support their impressive height.
There was something oddly organic about the tapering
cluster of rippled towers that reminded me of a Gaudi cathe-
dral or a rock formation sprouting from a New Mexico
canyon.

Jeff bit off the charred end of the hot dog and then
neglected the remainder. He was totally rapt. When the girls
came too close he waved them back impatiently. The main
construction complete, he proceeded to carve out niches

with his index finger and dribble abstract gargoyle shapes and rainspouts. His hands worked deftly, and watching him amused me, but the girls needed a nap. They were becoming weepy. Even slathered in high-SPF sunscreen, their skin had absorbed too much light. They radiated heat; they glowed ominously. So I carried them back to the cottage. I stripped off their swimsuits and laid them down, and the three of us drowsed in the wavering shadows of the pine trees that shimmered in the window frames.

By nightfall, all but a few of the most ambitious builders had finished their creations. Jeff and I made shish kebabs on the grill, popped the girls into sweatshirts, and wended our way down to the beach through the darkness. Pit fires gnawed through piles of driftwood, and people wormed around under blankets. The flames traced orange-and-black patterns on the sand. Strange shrill whoops sounded in the distance. The girls wanted to walk, so I took Patrice by the hands, and Jeff took Caitlin, and we let them lead us. We inched across the sand, stride by stride, pausing only to swing them over a mounded pile or an unexpectedly long-reaching wave. To our right dark miles of empty water met the sky at an invisible juncture. Up ahead in the distance, the lighthouse swung its beam out and around in a centrifugal motion. Across the lake, en route to Escanaba, a freighter heeded the light and gave the shore wide berth.

Jeff turned away from the water and looked out over the shapes of the sand structures—buttresses, pinnacles, arches, courtyards, and drawbridges—that wobbled in the firelight.

We tried to make out the sculptures. "Is that Bach?" He pointed to a lumpy form at our right.

"I think it's Elvis," I said. We were silent, then resumed our slow pace, passing one marker at a time.

"You know, it's really very beautiful," Jeff said, and I opened my mouth to point out the banality of his adjective, when Patrice let out a piercing scream.

Down on the sand at our feet a dark shape, long as my leg, stretched out just barely beyond the water's reach. It was dead and had been for a long time; the inky skin torn away in patches, and the sharp outline of its fins pressed flat into the sand, but the way the tail curved back on the spine, and the gape of its broken triangular jaw, teeth bared, gave it a terrible three-dimensionality. A livid eye glowered sightlessly up at us in the inconstant light. The skin on the back of my neck tightened. Something like that, I thought—it came like a nightmare from an alien depth far away and was better left to itself—something like that should not see the light of day.

"What the hell," Jeff said. Caitlin picked up the alarm and wailed along with Patrice, although I don't think she knew at what or why. Patrice shrieked and flailed as if she were being electrocuted. I could barely hold her. Her scream trilled painfully along my nerves and vibrated in my eardrums with not even a pause for breath.

Clutching Caitlin to his chest, Jeff took a few cautious steps and bent as if to better examine the thing. "Don't," I yelled over the screams twining around each other and amplifying. "Don't go near it, Jeff, whatever it is." The hysteria was catching.

"I just want to—" He propped Caitlin next to my knee, and I almost dropped Patrice on top of her in my attempt to disentangle myself, to catch him, to pull him back.

"Jesus Christ." He batted away my hand without turning. "It looks like it slithered up—that's the worst—" The lighthouse beam swept over us in a wash, then plunged us into the dark.

I put my hand down and groped around for two heads, and when I did, I came up one short. "Jeff," I said. I spoke so calmly and quietly I could barely hear myself. I had to force myself to say his name again, more loudly. A few feet away something unseen splashed into the water.

"Just a sec," he said. When he turned and looked back the beach lit up blindingly again and told me what I already knew: Patrice had vanished.

In two slow-motion strides Jeff had reached and then passed me, heading down the beach at a run, flinging up sand with each step, retracing the churn of our footprints. He had his hands cupped to his mouth, bellowing Patrice's name. I picked up Caitlin and followed. She was compliant even in her agitation, clinging tightly to me as she sobbed, but she weighed me down, strangling me with the collar of my windbreaker, slowing me to one stride for every three of Jeff's. I could only fall back and watch helplessly from a distance.

He finally caught her, but not before she slipped through a gap in the sand pile and plunged into the midst of all that fragile architecture. For someone so tiny, a person still learning the physics governing her movements, her rampaging looked purposeful, deliberate. She held out her arms, and the buttresses, ramparts, and drawbridges of our fellow contestants crumbled in her wake. Jeff's castle folded in on itself. The light came and raced away again. Jeff's elbow struck a mass, clumps of sand sprayed into the air, and the loose grains, carried by the wind, stung my eyes. I could hear my husband's curses hissing in the air.

Jeff plucked up Patrice from the western hemisphere. She'd fallen, I think, into the Pacific Ocean and created a crater that sucked in the coast of California. There were still tears streaked on her face, but she wasn't crying; she was all done with that. I held out my free arm to her, but she only rubbed her knuckles against her eyes and turned stonily away from me.

Sandy rubble lay all around us. But nothing could be done, and so we left it and trudged on, trailing Caitlin's plangent cries down the beach, past the bluffs where the empty frames of empty houses loomed just above our heads, hidden on the brink. Jeff might know a word for this, a precise and spare phrase to describe the point where everything hangs precariously in the balance, waiting to stay put or to fall, but then maybe he wouldn't, so I didn't ask, and we continued to make our way, step by step, through the dark.

THE PLACE OF THE HOLY

A S A GIRL I USED to walk through the tree branches when the storms were coming in. The oaks pitched in the wind; the limbs came and went under my feet. My untied shoelaces stung my ankles and my hair blew straight up in electric tentacles while the updrafts sped up the trunks and carried the loose leaves skyward and away. The world's alignment disappeared; overhead the clouds churned in a lurid flickering light and below me, past the open space, the grass flattened in sheets and then bristled up in a strangely drugged motion, slow for all the air raging through it. The wind soughed through the woods, and every chink of space filled with a clamor like a cacophony of violins.

The first time my mother caught me at this, she asked me not to do it anymore. She worried about someone seeing me skipping recklessly across the empty air in the rising gale, my skirt blown up around my hips. A farmer, maybe, heading for shelter. Those men were not such a laconic breed as they seemed. She said nothing about the possibility of my falling, and I knew even then that she understood the precise nature of the feat and all its complex laws of equilibrium, how it could come with no more difficulty than crossing a balance beam, one foot in front of the other. I'd seen her behind the rhododendrons when the air stopped and the sky began lowering over the Ozarks, dancing in tight little steps that she thought no one saw. Her heavy braid bounced from one shoulder to the other, and the constrained intricacy of her footwork did not disguise her urgency as if to remain still any longer might be the death of her. I continued climbing the trees, but I did not let her catch me again.

I was too young to remember when my parents bought the Place of the Holy, an old revival house that sat up in the hills of northwestern Arkansas. Nor do I recall how they once worked on it together, arresting the decay that came from a decade of neglect, breaking the two conjoined halls into two stories that contained five large bedrooms and installing two bathtubs and a new gas stove. My father built our wraparound porch with his own two hands. I once saw a photograph of him my mother must have taken, standing in our kitchen knee-deep in plumbing, oblivious of the camera and frowning to himself, although I haven't seen that picture in years, and I'm no longer really sure it exists.

Sometime after that, though, my father began spending a great deal of time in Utah and Colorado where he was dropped out of airplanes into forest fires. His trips home to Arkansas were infrequent and brief, no longer than two weeks—just enough time for his singed eyebrows to lighten again and his hands to shed their scabs and regain their smooth red-and-tan marbling. He told me stories of heat so intense that it warped the air, exploded trees, and evaporated entire streams into nothing. Then he was gone again. He did not like it there with us, I believe, and the women my mother started taking in shortly after the house was finished. When he was home he tried to ignore them, bowing his head as he passed through the dining room on his way out to mow the lawn. If he did happen to glance up, his eyes would lock on one of them and linger too long, as if he were trying to work out an irritating problem. He wished to God they would just get some gumption, he said to my mother, who turned a deaf ear toward him. She disregarded most of what he said, and I breathed easier when he was gone.

My mother taught me at home until it was time for me to go to the high school in Fayetteville. In the summers, she took a break from schooling me, and I helped her run the house. Year in and year out, summer remained the busiest season. "The heat," my mother said, "wears on everyone; it will always make the violence worse." For my own part, I think it has something to do with the long days, all those wakeful hours, all those seconds with your eyes wide open, so much time for the intolerable facts to burn their impression inside of you. People will reach a breaking point; they will turn and run.

And those women found their way to us. Often they came late at night or very early in the morning. My mother installed a light on the back porch and left it burning from dusk until dawn, shining through a murky halo of insects. She slept with her window propped up so she could hear the faintest steps, those shifting with indecision on our threshold, those ready to turn back into the darkness. She was a light sleeper, and she slept best alone.

The summer I turned thirteen I had bruised shins and the sinewy strength of a skinny adolescent boy, so I took on the chores of my absent father. I pushed the mower around the clearing our house sat in, executing sharp turns with a practiced twist of my shoulders, shearing the tufted heads off the clover, and sucking careless bumblebees into the whirling blades. I twiddled the wires of the generator, splaying the frayed ends with my fingernails and patiently braiding them back together, time and time again, until the machine pulsed to life. I slithered up and down the steep pitch of our roof, scooping the gleaming black slime out of the gutters and hammering their loose ends back into shape. There was a woman named Verna who had come to us the beginning of that May, and she seemed to dislike me. *I can see your panties, little girl,* she called up to me from the yard as I skipped, unafraid, across loose shingles that trembled under my steps. *You'd best watch yourself, you're getting too old for that.*

I was perched up there one morning in June, searching out the source of a leak that had begun troubling the sleepers on the second floor when I saw Reverend Harry for the first time. I rested the hammer against my bare kneecap and watched as his car rocked gently over the ruts in our driveway and came to a stop. He got out and came up the walk. All around me the birds wove their bright and monotonous songs. Even from the roof, I could tell he was a tall man. His dark hair lifted in the wind, and he approached with loose and unhurried strides. A few feet in front of the house he stopped and raised his eyes, searching, one hand lifted as if in a salute. His gaze startled me; I had thought myself hidden by the jutting edge of the dormer window. The sun must have nearly blinded him, but he stood patiently squinting into the skyline trying to make out what would reveal itself to him. He wished me a good morning and I did not respond: I stood firmly in familiar heights, and he was an uninvited stranger. I lifted one bare foot to scratch the other ankle, a gesture my mother called slovenly, while I looked down at him.

My incivility didn't appear to faze him in the least. As if I had just reciprocated his pleasantries he said yes, he found the day delightful as well, his name was Reverend Harry, and then he inquired after the whereabouts of my mother.

"She's out," I said. That was a lie. My mother had been napping when I left the house. She'd been up very late the night before with our newest arrival, a middle-aged woman named Darlene, making her tea and talking to her late into the night. Darlene's sobs tore irregular little rents in the quiet house; they continued long after the talking had ceased, quiet sounds, but once we heard them none of us were able to sleep. I felt slightly light-headed with weariness, and every now and then the landscape would wrinkle around me, and I had to put out a hand to steady myself.

"Oh, now," said the Reverend Harry. "Are you sure you didn't make a mistake? I thought I saw someone moving around in there just as I was coming up the walk."

I shrugged. "We have a lot of people living in our house. Doesn't mean it was her."

"So I heard," he said. He stretched out his arms and began to fold up his shirtsleeves without taking his eyes off me. "Well, maybe I'll just have a seat on the porch and wait here for her to return if that's all right with you."

"Suit yourself." I swung the hammer over my shoulder manfully and tried not to flinch as the sharp points of it bit into my back. "I can't stop you."

He disappeared under the eave beneath me, and I heaved a sigh and set about looking for the leak again. It took me only five more minutes of searching to find it, a marshy patch stripped of shingles, probably in the last storm, that gave under the weight of my heel. My foot punched through nearly to the ankle, but I caught myself at the last second and bent to inspect the scratches that ringed my leg in strings of red beads. Out loud to no one in particular I spoke my mother's favorite phrase, *troubles always come in droves*, and loved the philosophical inflection it lent my voice. Far off in the distant hills, a shot was fired, and on cue the black-birds flooded the air. I felt the ripple of their passing wings like fingers in my hair.

In the minds of some Christian theologians the ties between the trouble and sin are infinite and inextricable, veins and arteries to a heart, little substantive difference between the coming and going, only suffering suffusing everything. I suppose that's why the preachers sniffed us out, a couple every season, spending a few days before they were off hunting again. To someone with an eye for sorrow our house must have given off its own glow, visible like a hearth in those sparsely populated hills. No wonder, then, that those eager to bestow the comfort of God came to us from miles around.

Let them come, my mother said. She herself did not believe a word spoken by those men, but some of the women staying with us did, and she thought it wouldn't hurt us to bow our heads in accordance to the customs of our neighbors. She said maybe it would help them talk about us less. Not likely, but we can only do what we can do.

When I finally finished fixing the roof, replacing the rotten board and tacking down the gritty shingles over it as tight as scales, Reverend Harry was no longer on the front porch. I pushed open the front door and entered the house with a sense of trepidation. The interior gloom rose to greet me; I groped for the screen behind me. "There you are," said my mother. Reverend Harry sat at the end of the long dining room table, a cup of coffee in front of him, and my mother sat in the chair next to him. They both jumped, just slightly, when the door closed behind me. All the other chairs were pushed in tight; dinner would not be served for another hour, and the maple stripes of the butcher's block, not yet covered in place settings, gleamed in the floral light drifting through curtains. The scabs had begun to stiffen around my ankle like a manacle. I shuffled restlessly in the doorway, crossing and uncrossing my sticky arms, breathing in the smell of myself and wishing I weren't.

"We've found her," said Reverend Harry in a voice that carried an undertone of meaning to me, although when he smiled at me I could see no malice in it. Our sturdy blue coffee mug seemed diminished by the breadth of his large hands. With one finger, he twirled the handle in a slow and steady revolution; the opaque liquid in the center remained undisturbed like an unblinking eye.

"Did you hurt yourself?" My mother smoothed her hair and stood up, gesturing with the dish towel to my leg. "I told you to wear shoes up there. You're going to give yourself tetanus."

"I forgot."

"Good Lord." She turned to Reverend Harry. "If she weren't so handy, I'd have packed her off a long time ago." Her use of the third person, as if I were not in the room watching them, filled me with a sudden distrust. I stood very still, waiting.

He gave a laugh. "Looks like she earns her keep, though."

They both turned to study me, sizing me up. Dirty, wounded, and outnumbered, I sensed an allegiance into which I could not enter. So I childishly dropped the hammer to the floor. It thundered down against the hardwood beneath my feet. Then I raced up the stairs, taking them two at a time in graceless strides. Even in my haste, I made out my mother's startled gasp. "I had no idea . . ." she began, but

I sliced off the end of her sentence cleanly when I slammed the door behind me.

I stayed up in my room, sulking, wishing to be outside in the world, but believing my seclusion would impress my mother more than the sight of my disappearing back as I rambled off into the woods, which I did most every afternoon. I sat on my bed fitfully turning the pages of one of her books of poetry. Byron wondered where the weary eye should repose—mine rested on the windowsill, watching the sun's angle widen there as the day dwindled away. My pointed retreat must have had some effect because she did not call me down to help with setting the table. Perhaps she was afraid I would refuse, and then a scene would ensue. I pressed my ear to the floorboards, and each step of those gathering to break bread seeped into my ear. My mother knocked briskly twice on my door then a hesitant third time as if to make amends, but I remained where I lay, listening, and after a few minutes, she went away again.

For a time, I slept there dry-mouthed on the floor, the sounds of the meal still trickling up into my head making me dream of ham slices, crumbs scattering, and lemonade quivering in water glasses.

When I opened my eyes, dusk had draped blue shadows across every surface in the room. I could hear a man's voice below me coming through the open window. I was stiff and hungry, and for almost a minute I attached it to no one. I simply listened to its sonorous cadences, its crescendos and hushed falls. It spoke to me of affliction and anguish. The melancholy insistence of the repetitions, the persistent lapping of clauses in the growing dark turned these abstractions into something suffocating and ominous. I sat up quickly, and only then did I remember Reverend Harry.

My head wouldn't turn straight on my stiffened neck; I was forced to sidle along the stairs, feeling each one out with my feet without looking down. I tried not to make a sound, but Clarice heard me. Clarice, my favorite of all the women. Clarice, six months pregnant with a nose mashed by her husband beyond repair. Clarice, who breathed in and out of her mouth so that her every movement was accompanied by a troubled sigh. A month earlier, with my mother's help, she had finally filed for divorce, but she still wore her engagement ring, and sometimes she let me wear it around the house where I flashed it in all the windows.

She was the only one not out on the lawn listening to the reverend. Even my mother, who normally avoided these sermons, preferring to scuttle back into the kitchen and bang the pots around together, had joined the group outdoors. She was not sitting in the grass with the other women but standing on the porch steps, one foot resting on the stair behind her, poised in the act of descending or turning while her fingers traced inscrutable shapes on the railing beneath her hand. The wooden beam her head rested against had snagged a few loops of her hair, and the shining threads trailed along the grain. The window between us was latched, so I could no longer hear the reverend, but I could see him pacing slowly as he spoke, stepping through the grass with measured strides. He held out his arms expansively to the twilight and then squatted to hold gently the faces of the women who watched him, one then another, speaking intently to each in her turn. The rising shadows hid his expression—who could know what private consolation he was delivering? Then he rose to his full height again, white shirt glowing, while the fireflies throbbed and subsided at his feet.

Behind me, Clarice rocked herself in the chair next to the neglected piano—no one but my father knew how to play the instrument, and it sat silent while he was away, slowly going out of tune. She pushed off with one foot and then the other. "Come here, my darling," she said. I knelt on the floor, and she slowly kneaded away the knots in my neck, neither of us saying a word, just listening to her labored breathing. From time to time, she paused to touch her swollen stomach, confirming something, before she resumed once more. Finally, when I could drop my chin to my chest again, she leaned forward and whispered in my ear, "Your mother left your dinner on the table. Go on, there's no shame in eating it."

I rose stiffly to my feet and went to seek out this peace offering. I was ravenous and so parched by then that I could not have uttered a word if I tried.

That night, my mother was awoken by a knock on the screen door. I was sleeping hard, toiling my way through some uneasy dream, so I did not hear it. Only the sound of steps on the stairs and then a hand on my doorframe woke me, two quick knocks, my mother's signal to me. I rose without a thought, still fumbling after a vague glimmer that eluded me more with every step.

The dazzling kitchen yawed before my slitted eyes. A woman hunched at the small counter where my mother prepared our meals, her face hidden in her bloody hands, speaking in tongues. She was no one we had seen before. I stared stupidly at the red lining in her cuticles, crescents so thin and delicate they looked as if they had been etched in deliberately. "Shh . . ." my mother said over and over. She was trying to pull the woman's dirty blond hair back to see something. "I need you to get some gauze," she said to me. "Be quiet. Don't wake him." Meaning Reverend Harry, the only *him* in the house, bedded down on the sofa in our front room, no doubt feigning sleep.

I knew where the rolls of gauze lay in the back corner of the linen closet, could find them by touch. They unfurled and streamed through my fingers in shockingly white ribbons as I raced through the hallway back into the kitchen.

"She'll be all right," my mother said to me, reaching to take a roll without looking up. She lifted the woman's chin to the light. "Move your eyes to the left. Good. Now move them to the right."

"I took the car," the woman said. "He'll come after me. I took the car."

"Never mind that. It will all work itself out," my mother answered. She pulled out a chair and sat down. Still she didn't look away from the woman's face; something she saw there worried her. "Go wet this down, Nina." She stretched out an unused strip of gauze to me. "You can clean off her hands, at least."

The three of us huddled there together then, under the stark overhead glare of the kitchen light. I knelt at the woman's knees, wiping her fingers with the wet gauze, wiping away the rusty seams in her skin one stitch at a time. There were so many of those intricate crevices, the whorls across each knuckle, the webbing across each palm, the hidden crevices beneath each joint. I traced each one as though in a trance, the way you follow footprints in drifted snow, blindly, looking only one step ahead, never lifting your eyes. Crimson bloomed and spread in smears across the gauze clenched in my fist. The feeling drained from my feet, then from my ankles, then from my calf muscles.

Somewhere overhead my mother worked. Her body, as it leaned back and forth, cast flickering eclipses across the light. Over and over again, the woman kept saying the words, "I took the car," but neither of us responded, and eventually the repetition rendered the sounds mindless and empty like the shuddering ceiling fan that counted out the seconds until dawn.

In addition to the work of her beloved poets, my mother had in her possession a few outdated anatomy textbooks, their library markings scraped away by fingernail scratches. We perused them repeatedly throughout the duration of my homeschooling—she firmly believed that knowledge begins with a person's comprehension of their own unglamorous essence. By the age of thirteen I knew that the cochlea curls like a seashell that absorbs noise. I knew that capillaries are no thicker than hairs, that they filter blood into the most hidden parts of ourselves, that bones are threaded through with wormholes of empty space.

They are not fragile as you might believe—it takes a fair amount of force to break them. A blow can fall so quickly, though. The doing is so swift, the undoing so slow and so painstaking. Somehow, by some exertion of sheer will, by some sublime understanding, my mother sealed up wounds, aligned fractures, sent the pooling blood coursing back where it should go. The contusions dried up and evaporated like puddles; the bones settled into place like the dropping of drawbridges. My mother barely breathed as she worked; afterward her skin looked strangely gray as though part of her had leached away during her undertaking.

There was a limit to what she could do. When at last she sighed and settled back in her chair, the damaged woman's face appeared whole but swollen as if with edema, her skin stretched shiny under the strain.

I had seen this many times and had never once thought to be awed. I gently drooped my head against the healed woman's knee and started to close my burning eyes, but then I stopped. The doorway just beyond my shoulder was dark, but someone stood there, and I knew it was not one of the women. A beat passed, one more blink, one more rotation of the fan overhead, one more utterance, *I took the car*, and his form sharpened—arms crossed, hair rumpled from a restless sleep, lips parted, dumbfounded—perhaps from a dream that had not yet dissipated.

I looked up at my mother. She did not meet my eyes. Her pale brown hair was loose; unbraided, it spilled down into her lap, and she seemed preoccupied with tracing the path of its waving ends. She was wearing the same green nightgown she always wore, one washed to a translucent film, but that night she'd covered it with a brown sweater. Only a verdant glimpse could be seen from beneath it, a fold that clung to her damp collarbone like a leaf. She was too warm, of course, not pale at all, but flushed as if she'd lingered too long in the setting sun that evening. Her downturned face held an almost stricken expression. For the first time then, I understood that someone might find her beautiful. I reached out and beseechingly laid my hand on hers, but she did not seem to feel it. Instead, she turned her head and stared with great deliberation into the night that swarmed along the window. Moths tapped against the screen. They beat on and on, sounding like hands coming to claim something that did not belong to them.

I heard the two of them talking afterward. I lingered in the upstairs bathroom, running my fingers under the faucet, twisting the handles in turn, so the water first scalded, then froze the backs of my hands. Their voices were pitched low; it was difficult to separate the words from the pauses. The car needed to go back immediately—they concurred on that point—but they couldn't seem to agree on how it should be done. I strained to hear over the blurring effect of the water.

Every time I turned the tap to quiet it they lowered their voices again. *They always say that*, my mother said. *They always think someone is going to come after them. Usually they're wrong. It's a fear that's carefully cultivated.*

I don't like the thought, just you and, if, what will you do? The Reverend's baritone voice sank faster than my mother's, pieces dropping out of his sentences.

They've come before, said my mother, *I'll deal with this one too.*

It's not, my conscience, think, Caroline, little girl.

I could hear nothing more. I took a step toward the door as lightly as possible and suddenly my mother appeared from around the corner. "Go to bed, Nina," she said.

"It's almost morning."

"Go to bed." Her hands shook as she lifted them to gather her hair back, clearing it away and twisting it in a tightening coil as if she were girding up for battle. Her foot pursued its own separate and anxious beat on the floor, up and down, up and down, up and down.

"What is the matter with you?" I said, but she didn't answer.

"Go to bed. Emma's sleeping in the south room with Clarice. I had her take a sedative, and she's going to be fine."

I slapped the doorframe with my hand. "Bullshit." The deliberate obscenity was an attempt to call her back, to make her see reason, but she didn't rise to the occasion. Instead she turned. The shoes were already on her feet, laces cinched tight.

"I put the shotgun next to the table," she said. "You know

the drill. If someone comes to the door and he won't go away, shoot him."

I slept fitfully for almost two hours only to be awakened by sunlight roasting me slowly beneath the damp covering of my sheets. I went to the window and looked out. There was no sign of Reverend Harry's car, only my mother's decrepit pickup. Someone downstairs tapped plates together. I thumped down the stairs on my heels, pausing on each step before descending to the next.

It was only Clarice. She'd propped the Remington against the windowsill in order to set the table. I absently traced my fingertips along the smooth barrel, listening to the rasp of water heating in the teakettle. It sounded like a crowd exulting in the distance. Neither of us said a word until Clarice broke the silence. "Don't touch that thing," she said. "It makes me nervous."

I dropped my rebuked hand into its pocket. We both stood with our ears cocked for the popping of stones in the driveway. No one else was awake but us. Every now and then a bed creaked in one of the back rooms when someone turned over, and we lifted our heads, waited, then resumed our separate meditations as if they were serious work to be carried out.

At last we heard it. Clarice came rushing up behind me to the window. Her belly crushed me painfully to the glass. Reverend Harry's gray Chevy slowed to a stop. It took them a long time to get out of the car. My mother held up her head with one hand. She looked profoundly weary, the fever of the previous night utterly burnt out. The reverend followed her up the porch stairs. Two steps up she fumbled her footing, and he reached out a quick hand to steady her, but she righted herself before he could touch her.

"Thank God!" Clarice rejoiced as they came in through the door. She flung out her arms to them. "You had Nina and me here on the rack. I was beginning to think we might have to come after you. And she would have to drive because I don't think I can fit behind the wheel anymore."

I didn't say a word. I picked up the gun and took out the shells, standing them up on either side of the vase of lilacs Clarice had placed in the center of the table. One, then the other, very meticulously, as cool as if I were lining up forks. No one said anything, and I did not look up. The reverend shuffled his feet on the linoleum and cleared his throat. When I was finished, I snapped back the barrel with a resounding *click*. Then I gently laid the shotgun back on the windowsill and left the house, careful not to let the screen door slam behind me.

Slowly, over the course of the afternoon, the sky took on weight. From my vantage point, high at the top of my favorite oak tree, I set down my book and watched it ripen like a bruise, deep plum streaked with livid greens. You could not hallucinate something so vivid. Off in the distance, the Christ of the Ozarks stretched out his pristine white arms over the swelling landscape brushing the silky wind that rushed over the trees. From the direction of the house the piano started up. The sound of it arrested my breath, and then I realized that the player could be no one but the reverend. His fingers marshaled the notes with unhesitating precision into the sultry air. The strengthening breeze blew them straight to me, long lingering notes at first, then a collection of chords that picked up speed and leaped across octaves. Above me, the architecture of the clouds grew taller and more elaborate, shot through with small gold sidelights.

I watched the rain working its untroubled way southward to where I sat. When at last it began to fall around me, I laid aside my book. I stood and made my way across the branches, first deliberately and then more quickly until I was almost running. The limbs sprang away under my steps. My wet skin prickled with the electricity in the air; sheets of water poured over me. I could barely see. I thought I might be glowing like those luminous animals that live in the depths of an ocean I had never seen. Each step across empty space exhilarated me. I flung up my arms and felt the rain race through my fingers and fall away.

I ran on and on, but inevitably my headlong rush brought me home. I caught sight of Emma, alone on the porch. Her impassive face still did not look right, but that would take time. She watched me walk slowly across the bubbling grass, and as I brushed past her to go indoors, she snatched my slick wrist and gripped it tightly. With the sky emptying out endlessly over our heads, I could not understand what she said to me and asked her to repeat herself. I barely caught it the second time. She said, "Tell me how you do it."

The inside of our house was dark as a cave and almost as quiet. The walls of the entryway receded upward and away into the gloom, and above my head shadows swam across the pane of the rose window. Each drop that fell from the ends of my fingers seemed distinct from the one before. The seconds were slowing down, the giddy rush ebbing out quickly and a weak and empty hunger seeping in to take its place. I knew I might faint and felt dimly surprised by the lack of interest that accompanied the realization.

I did not faint. I reached out and wrapped my arms around the newel post of the staircase and waited. There was noise after all; I heard it now, the sound of a voice I had not heard at first over the ragged insistence of my own breathing.

My eyes adjusted and gradually I could see through the doorway into the sitting room, where I could discern the frozen shapes of the five women my mother had taken in from death. A quick death or slow, but a certain one. Clarice, Verna, Darlene, Mary Ann, and Jessica—they sat like stone statues in a garden listening to the reverend in still postures, waiting for the moss to overtake them, to encroach upon their lips and cheekbones and cover them over.

I had not immediately realized that he was talking because he was not standing. Instead, he was sitting on the piano bench, shirtsleeves rolled back, elbows propped on the opened case, legs stretched out. He spoke a few words, and then he paused for a long moment, thinking his own thoughts. In these stretches, without turning, he dropped a finger and meditatively tapped a note, once, twice, and then another. He might have been talking to himself; the room might have been empty. His eyes wandered across the wallpaper following the delicate spore pattern that trailed shadowy lines from floor to ceiling until his gaze reached the doorway and passed through it. I think they paused for a moment on me, standing there shivering with a sudden and unexpected chill. He kept watching, not saying a word, just hitting a black key, a plaintive D-sharp over and over.

Then he resumed speaking again, telling us of Job, perhaps his favorite book in the Bible. We should read the words for ourselves, he urged us, and think of their power, think of their beauty. *He cometh forth like a flower, and is cut down: he fleeth also as a shadow, and continueth not.* Think of that.

He reached out his hand and struck the lowest note on the keyboard. It resonated, too deep to even be a note really, a vowel without breath behind it. As its reverberations sank away, I turned my head and looked out the window to where a shape was passing us by. It was my mother. Her feet were bare, and her head was bent to watch them rise and fall through the wet grass, each step throwing muddied droplets up onto the hem of her skirt. She seemed, at first glance, to have no destination, and then I saw the basket against her hip and understood she meant to collect the clothes beaten from the line by the storm.

"To be cut down," continued the reverend, "our beauty so fragile, our time in the light so brief, and by what? What hand cuts us down? Our own. Our own sin. The savageness of those who do not understand the truth of things. Sorrow comes for us all. Think of Job—the upright, the pious— trouble came even to him. It came with the first footfalls of his servant who arrived and said, 'I only am escaped alone to tell thee.'"

He fell quiet again, thinking, until finally he continued. "I don't know, lately it strikes me that there are days when sorrow and weakness are like a hand at your elbow guiding you into the darkness, into places you can't foresee or prepare for. These places have their own allure that seems like beauty, but it is false. Don't stay there, don't linger. Turn to God. Find your way out."

Again a silence, a clear middle C. No one breathed. Then I heard the screen open very softly behind me and the smell of the rain drifted in. My mother's shadow fell across my peripheral vision and stayed there.

Reverend Harry leaned hard on his last and final note, holding it until it bled out and only the empty and dissonant undertone of disturbed air remained. The sky had begun to lighten in the windows and I could see the indigo crescents that underscored his eyes. "We are not given answers in this life," he said. "The wash of light, the chorus of angels is only a promise we hope for, but right now there are only the smallest glimpses of grace around us, sparks hidden in the grit. We can only do the best we can and . . ."

At last he looked up at my mother, although I knew he'd sensed her there from the moment she came in the door. "Am I correct, Caroline?"

We all turned to gape at her then, emptied like bats out of the lonely towers of our reveries. Everyone looked startled except for Clarice, who frowned as if she knew an answer that made her sad. My mother was still resting her basket on her hip; all those wet clothes heaped inside of it must have been almost more weight than her arms could hold. "You tell me," she said finally. "You're the one who carries the Word of God." She hoisted up the basket with both arms; the effort caused her voice to quaver. "Excuse me," she said. Then she turned and left us there.

I could not sleep that night. I lay in bed, feeling my heart beat into the crook of my arm. *He cometh forth like a flower.* On the other side of the wall, someone paced out one confined lap after another, maybe Clarice, maybe Emma. *He cometh forth like a flower and is cut down.* I did not understand the words and why, meaning nothing to me, the memory of them made my throat tighten. The thin line of light beneath my door vanished. After a while the footsteps became slower and slower as if the pacer did not intend to lie down but meant to walk even while she slept. Finally, I kicked off the covers. I stepped into my shoes, did not bother to tie them. They made no noise as I glided downstairs toward the door. As I passed the front room, I paused to look in, not daring to breathe. The sheets were stretched across the sofa. A pillow rested at one end and an extra blanket at the other, each touch a small charade, careful preparations for a sleeper who did not lie there. I stood listening for a sound. There was none, and so I moved on, passing through the front door. I did not shut it. I left the doorway clear for the insects or anything else in the night to enter behind me if it so wished.

The sky was dark, another storm was coming, but the air was still calm. It would not reach us for another hour yet. The immense air masses were still battling their way across the hills, unseen, but they were coming for us. A few stars still cast out palsied beams that revealed the yard as I knew by heart but the edges to all the familiar shapes—the trees, the flowerbeds, the hammock, the clothesline flecked with pins—were now lost to my gaze. My shoe kicked against a stone. I bent down and, with a small amount of effort, worked it loose from the clotted earth. It was as large as my fist and dense as a miniature planet. I wrapped my fingers around it and slowly it sapped away the warmth from them.

Carrying it with me, that new heft beneath the knuckles of my right hand, was like gaining a sudden infusion of strength. I swung the stone past my hip like a pendulum. I stepped into the peonies. I broke their stems and turned their dark-hearted faces to the dirt with my feet, blotted the color out of them.

From the bed of ruined flowers, I could turn my head up and see the second-story window behind which my mother slept. The light was on but only a dim one; it came from the lamp by her bed. And I heard the sound of a voice, not hers, but the reverend's. I could not make out the words, only the cadence, the one he had used that afternoon, soft and halting and pained. Then I realized that he was saying her name, "Caroline, Caroline," over and over.

I didn't think at all, not one thought. The arc of that stone was lovely, a streaking white parabola issued from the span of my arm like the single sweep of an unearthly wing. At its apex it hung for a moment as if I might still be redeemed. Then the window burst into shards, a shattering as irreparable and complex as lightning. Tiny slivers blew away and fell down around me like knives while I listened to the sound of the impact ring on in my ears.

I did not move. I knew they were coming for me, and so I stood there and waited with the calm that descends upon you when waiting is all that is left to do.

The reverend was faster out of the house than my mother. I saw him charge through the back door, throwing it out of the way with the bulk of his shoulders behind his rigid arms. "It shouldn't happen like this," I heard myself say to my mother somewhere in the darkness behind him and maybe the other women, fluttering around her like moths. "It shouldn't happen like this."

I couldn't say anything else. He seized me by the scruff of the neck and drove me down. He was so strong. My feet lost their hold on the earth; I was airborne, and then I fell, my own sickening weight against the dirt. My teeth clashed together. The last of the stars blacked out. In the distance my mother sang out a shrill dirge for me. Gravel bit into my cheekbone. I opened my eyes, and the flecks glittered around me, but what light they were reflecting I do not know. I was thinking of my father then, the stories he told of falling into smoke so dark it was like being devoured. He didn't breathe the whole time, he said. He simply waited out the eternal seconds until he had passed through it, reached the bottom, and could begin to make his way across the forest floor, until he could look up above him and see the brittle branches burning overhead, every limb, every stem, every tiny twig, every one of them, thousands upon thousands, illuminated with a heartbreaking and exquisite flame.

THE ART OF FALLING

AT A QUARTER TO SIX, Kevin Cass begins his day on the roof of an eighteen-story building. After he gauges the speed of the wind (ten miles an hour from the southeast) he pauses to look out over the city of Vancouver, the predictable grid of its streets, right angles and parallels converging just before the Canadian horizon. At his feet tiny red suns blaze in the windshields of a dozen cars that speckle the gray plain of a parking lot. Up in the heights of the city, away from the heat of the pavement, the breezes brush coolly by, strained through his outstretched fingers. Kevin straightens, lifts his chin, inhales twice, and jumps. Three and a half seconds later the air cushion blossoms up around him. He sinks down, opening his eyes in time to see the sky disappear into the yellow folds and then spread out overhead again like a gauzy stain. He exhales. Efficient hands reach down and bat away the bright plastic billows, clearing a space for him to stand.

They want the shot again. Assistants rush in to reset the nets and cameras, and Kevin walks to the corner stand to buy the *Times* and a coffee from a tired-looking man who stands behind stacks of newspapers thick with headlines. Before Kevin finishes the first few sips, they want him back up again. They're rushing through the takes; the director wants another one while the light still filters through the skyline at an acute angle, and a bloody red still suffuses the air. Kevin pours his cup out on the sidewalk; the coffee will be cold by the time he gets down to the ground to reclaim it. He strides off toward the hotel where he'll spend the next two hours jumping and falling.

This entails four more run-throughs and then a fifth jump that is not strictly necessary, but they have the time, and the director likes to *play it safe*. (The phrase is one of the man's motifs. He is without irony.) By the time Kevin reaches the roof for his final leap, the city is stirring, a gradual accretion of vehicles and bodies like thoughts collecting and struggling into momentum. Doors open and shut far below him in countless synaptic flurries. A cluster of observers has congregated along the perimeter of the movie set, faces tilted upward to witness his descent from the sky. The small gathering of them shines blandly up at him like coins, and he notices then from their golden cast that the portentous quality of the early-morning light is quickly dwindling away.

Kevin looks at them once, not again. He lines up his toes along the edge of the roof, that sharp right angle pressed tight against the emptiness of open space. A few seeds, somehow blown miraculously skyward, have taken root in the grit of the cement, and Kevin steps around the spindly plants with care, trying not to crush them with his feet. He stares straight down, chin to his chest, to the yellow target below him, crosshatched to a center, that very specific point in the universe he must strike and not miss. He fixes his eyes upon it, just for a moment, and then launches himself breathlessly outward and down.

No one really believes the stunt double will misgauge his jumps, that he will plummet to his death, be run over by the wheels of a cargo truck or a train, that his parachute will malfunction. Still, Kevin knows that the film crew and bystanders hold their breath while he's in the air. It seems to be a universal superstition: bracing for the unthinkable keeps it at bay. By withholding their exhalations they pay homage to the possibility of disaster, their helplessness in the face of it.

In the first half second of his fall, he knows something is amiss. He has miscalculated the speed of the wind, which has gained strength and amplified the updraft, or perhaps he dragged his legs in the push off. He should be upright, leading with his feet, but he is not. His body tilts; he feels the weight of his chest pitching forward, pulling his head down with it. He should see the sky. Instead, he sees the ground. Balconies, flowerpots, window washers, clouds, flicker between his knees. He does not know what he is headed toward. His arms swim easily through the insubstantial air, grasping for something—anything—he knows is not there.

As he hits the air cushion, he retches. For several seconds his body can neither draw in nor expel air, so he simply lies stunned in the suffocating nylon mesh that enfolds him.

After a minute one of the lighting assistants appears in his peripheral vision, leans over, and slaps him on the back a few times. "Man," he says, "your life must flash in front of your eyes whenever you do that kind of shit."

At last, at last, Kevin breathes out. Somewhere nearby the director raves about the flailing and uncontrolled quality of the fall, how spectacular, how much he loved it, and Kevin realizes then that not one of them understood anything was wrong. He wipes his lips with the back of his hand and swallows down the bitter taste in his mouth. "Not really," he says. And he climbs to his feet.

After that they're done with him. Kevin is free to buy brunch, to check out of his room, hail a cab, board a flight back to Los Angeles.

As he waits in the checkout line at the airport he thinks ahead to his next job, a stunt that will require him to hang glide into a landing on the roof of a Ford Explorer. The filming is almost a month away. He has four weeks of freedom ahead of him, a visit with his daughter, filled with activities he has painstakingly planned, but right now he cannot remember any of them. He shifts the strap chafing his collarbone and, before he can restrain himself, he sighs so heavily that the woman in front of him glances back and then steps forward pointedly as if he's just done something obscene. Kevin moves up and stares at the back of her head daring her to turn around and say something, but she does not.

Strangers brush past and each jostle against his elbow causes Kevin's teeth to clench. Somewhere behind him a toddler shrieks a shrill expression of delight, and the startling sound lingers painfully in his eardrums. As he looks around, he observes how the fluorescent lights cast stark shadows that relentlessly underline each irregularity, no matter how faint, on every face. They have all been waiting for so long, Kevin thinks, for days, for years, in some gray time zone—it's like seeing what the future will bring, and it will not be kind to any of them.

Even after he enters the confines of the plane and folds himself into the window seat he cannot relax. Every joint in his body aches. All those projecting bones—his heels, his elbows, his shoulders—they articulate the pain of decades of landings. Each one mumbles its own distinct complaint. Someday, they remind him, he will have to stop.

Not until the plane glides onto the runway and the acceleration of takeoff presses him into his chair—his body again in the grip of physical forces beyond his control—does Kevin think through the last fall of the morning, recalling that salty taste of panic in his mouth, and only against his will. Close calls are a requisite part of his work; he tries not to let them stay with him. The sooner the details fade away the better.

But the words spoken by the lighting assistant ring in his ears. People have expressed that cliché to him before. He supposes it could happen; he knows that the brain can work at astonishing speeds. He can't guess what those dying people see, what pattern the flicker of moments might create as they cascade down upon one another. It seems too much to hope for. Still, he has always thought it might be something unspeakably beautiful. All he remembers from this morning, though, is the sharpness of the light and the air passing between his fingers with a thin, almost slippery ease. Nothing else.

At the sound of a faint chime, Kevin shifts in his seat. The California landscape rises beneath him, becoming ever more complex the closer it comes. The flight is almost over, the wings of the plane now low enough to cast shadow blades upon the earth.

When he disembarks at LAX, Elizabeth is waiting for him, fresh off her own flight from New York. Her luggage sits at her feet, and she rests her chin on the knobby top of her cello case, watching passengers stream along, moving her eyes from left to right but not turning her head. Her hair is looped up into a messy knot and pastel crescents underscore her tired eyes, but it doesn't matter. Even in Los Angeles, land of the false and the beautiful, men and women turn their heads as they pass her by. It wasn't until Elizabeth began to grow up that Kevin realized that extraordinarily lovely people share the same fate as the deformed—the inability to travel through the world unnoticed. The flawless quality of her symmetry makes her as much of a freak as a man with a hook for a hand. When Kevin introduces her to his friends and colleagues, "Here's my daughter now," their heads snap back. They look again in disbelief.

He wonders what it must feel like and how much Elizabeth knows. Surely she must. The two of them have never discussed it.

She disentangles herself from the cello and embraces him.

"How was your flight?" Kevin shoulders her bag with his free arm, and she hefts her unwieldy instrument.

"Terrible," she says. She has been waiting for this question. "The woman next to me was absolutely certain we would never make it here. Halfway into the flight we hit some turbulence, and I had to hold her hand the rest of the way. I kept patting her head and saying, 'Shh, there, there.'" With her free arm she reaches up and brushes Kevin's thinning hair, demonstrating.

"Poor thing." Elizabeth's ease with people always startles him. She certainly did not acquire it from him.

"I hope you're referring to me."

"Of course. *There, there.*" He pats her shoulder and manages a small grin before he turns and glances around for an exit. "Let's find a cab and get the hell out of here."

He doesn't have a chance to really look at her again until they are settled into the taxi and hurtling along a congested freeway. She stares out through the scratches and smudges of the window, all eyes, then smiles when she sees him watching her.

"You miss it at all?"

She tips her head. "I forget how bright it is here," she says. "Even with the haze, you know? There's so much color." She looks away again. "I can't believe I didn't remember."

Kevin stares out past her profile. He has no idea what she's talking about.

By eight thirty they're home, bags dropped on the stones in the foyer, drinking wine out of glasses so large that the rims dig into the bridges of their noses when they tip them for the last dregs. Elizabeth sits like a little girl when she comes home, legs hanging over one arm of the chair, her long skirt wadded between her knees. After they open the second bottle of Pinot, after Elizabeth has determinedly steered the conversation through the fall program of the New York Philharmonic, the eccentricities of guest conductors, and the dissolute nature of brass players, there is a moment of silence. Kevin cautiously asks about her mother.

"She's fine," Elizabeth says. "Working on another book."

"Another book on *loving yourself*." Kevin whirls his wine; it almost slips over the edge. He calls Harriet a charlatan. If this hurts Elizabeth she doesn't give it away. She drops her gaze to her lap; he catches the twist of her half smile not meant for him, gone as soon as she looks up again.

"You might try reading one sometime," she says.

"Oh, oh." He settles back in his chair and raises his half-empty glass as if in a prelude to a toast. "Here it comes."

"No. I only have so much breath to waste." She runs a hand up and down along her forearm and sighs. "I've come to accept my limitations. I don't try to preach to the resigned."

Kevin's head is fuzzy. That expression is not correct, he knows, but the right word fails to present itself as it should. His eyes wander across the darkening windowpane in front of him as if they might somehow capture the phrase and pin it there against the slippery glass, but it eludes him, sliding away again and again until finally he gives up and lets it go.

"Talk to me." In her last syllable he catches an undertone, a huskiness to the long *e* that threatens to undermine the lightness of her mocking command. She clears her throat. "It's how this works, you know. Now that I've talked, you're supposed to tell me something. Something I don't know." She reaches out and fills her glass. "Tell me how the business of death-defying is going."

"Oh, it's going along, I suppose. Same old, same old." As he stares out into the accumulating dusk, Kevin feels the weight of the day taking shape in his chest, his headlong fall turning into words that rise and press up against his soft palate. But just as he opens his mouth he turns his head and catches a glimpse of her upturned face, bright as one of those careless bystanders', and he thinks, no, better not. So he shrugs his shoulders, tips his hand in a side-to-side motion and says nothing else.

"Succinct as ever, I see." With her fingernail she scratches at the suede upholstery covering her chair. "The other day I—"

"So tell me," Kevin interrupts. "Why the cello?" He's startled by his own question and its inflection—too quick, too earnest—and before it even dies away he regrets it. "I'm just curious, that's all."

She sets her glass on the end table between them and stares at him quizzically. "Why do I play? I don't know. Why do you jump off buildings?"

Kevin shifts impatiently. "It's not the same thing at all."

"I'm sorry. It's just—I'm not used to—" He watches the chase of thoughts flitting past, one after another, in the subtle workings of her features. "It's just strange hearing you ask the question. I wasn't prepared."

"Fair enough." Restlessly, he rolls his right arm around in its socket. The shoulder hurts the worst. He must have hit it coming down this morning.

Elizabeth laughs once—a flat sound—and swings her feet over the arm of the chair to the floor in a fluid motion of skirt and legs. "I'm cutting us off." She stands and lifts the glass from his hand, but she hesitates before she heads into the kitchen. "I think there's just *joy* in it," she says slowly. "Doing something—I don't know—unapologetically beautiful." She studies the picture hanging on the wall just above his head and does not meet his eyes. "You know what I mean?" A flush slips up her neck, then recedes, and she doesn't leave a space for his response. "I'm ready to keel over, Dad. I'll see you in the morning, okay?" And she slides through the doorway and disappears.

After his daughter climbs upstairs to bed (to dream about strings, to dream about fermatas, and the flash of bows under stage lights), Kevin turns out the lamps and roams stride by stride across the smooth floors in the dark, up and down the staircase. The vaulted ceilings vanish somewhere up above his head; the walls recede, and the corners startle him by leaping out like elbows to bring him up short, forcing him to turn.

His pacing brings him back into the living room. Floodlights radiating from the neighboring houses fill the space with their strange bright exhalations, and even with the lights off the outline of the chairs and tables remain distinct, each form trailing a diffuse shadow across the hardwood floor. From the middle of the room, he can almost discern the X-ray prints hanging on the opposite wall. Whenever Kevin looks at them he thinks about the stunt performers of seventy-five or a hundred years ago, the ones who performed without the air cushions, harnesses, and safety glass, before an era of health insurance. Those men were proud of their broken limbs and concussions, talismans of their courage, however misplaced. The whole science that Kevin has learned by heart—all those points where the body can absorb shock, the way it can maintain speed, hold a straight line against the wind, describe a trajectory, roll away the force of a landing—those men disregarded utterly. Clint Trucks, whose career came to a close not long after the invention of the X-ray, framed his own ghostly prints and hung them in his home for his visitors to admire. Kevin purchased the reproductions almost fifteen years ago, not long after his divorce.

He steps closer to examine them, trying to make them out for what they are rather than how he remembers them to be, studying the femurs and tibia. Unless you know their origins, the framed shapes are nothing more than striking abstractions—lean white lines swollen with burls where the bones have broken, then come back together again. An orthopedist once told Kevin that after a bone breaks and knits together, it thickens and becomes stronger than before. If that's true, Kevin thinks, those men who survived a decade of work must have had skeletons that were nearly unbreakable. His own would not compare so well.

At the sound of the ceiling creaking over his head, Kevin blinks, looks up from the planks beneath his feet. His gaze has fallen; he's been studying the cracks, running his eyes along the parallels as if the lines will reconcile themselves and come together. When Elizabeth was born, Kevin promised Harriet he would guard what he said to their daughter about his profession and keep the subjunctive to himself. There would be no hairsbreadths for Elizabeth, Harriet said, no narrow brushes or close escapes. Well, he has kept his word all right, although Harriet is now hundreds of miles away and will not know the difference. Let no one say he does not honor those agreements into which he enters.

A hot splinter of pain pulses once beneath his scapula and subsides. Kevin turns away, walks slowly down the hall, and climbs the stairs to bed.

He awakens at six thirty, later than he intends, to the vibrations of Elizabeth's practice seeping up through two floors and under the gap beneath his door. All he can hear in his bedroom are the high notes. The low ones dissolve into the studs and drywall despite how forcefully she strikes them.

They swell up around him, though, as he descends the stairs. She's playing in the front room, and Kevin pauses in the doorway to watch her. She doesn't look up, and he isn't sure if she realizes that he's there or not. The music broods like a dirge and then quickens—probably something nineteenth century. Schumann? Brahms? His ignorance is profound. The pins are slipping out of her blond hair; tendrils spill over her bowing arm, which churns, the sharp angle of her elbow thrusting in and out as if she is attempting to uproot a stone from the earth or bail herself out of an incoming tide. The dusky tones swirl together, bursting into high splashes that slide over a brink and slip away.

Kevin means to steal off so as not to distract her, but the inexorable momentum of the music holds him there waiting for the peak it strains toward. Notes rush forward, the following swelling up before the preceding fade, filling the air like a watery rise in the depths of a stone canyon, a skyward surge toward the expanse of a diluvial plain overhead.

Unable to stir he remains there, listening, his hands growing cold, his legs taking on weight. He knows this piece, has heard it somewhere before—the score to a yawing drop panning out at his feet, perhaps, or a song played at his wedding years ago. Or before that—the accompaniment to a stranger's hand pressed on his sleeve at a funeral for a passing he has forgotten until this moment. Or maybe the strains take him back even earlier—an afternoon in his infancy when he was left alone for the first time on the grass beneath an open window to watch the shadows fall through the leaves before the knowledge of the coming silence filled those resonances with sadness.

And finally she reaches it; her fingers slide along the neck of the cello, falling through octaves, reaching their position, and bearing down. They quiver under the strain, holding their arc like a breath, impossibly long, meting out the final low note, sustaining it, until its last tremors fade away.

In a tidy flourish she pulls off the bow, but she does not glance up. Sweat gleams in her collarbone. She breathes hard. When she shifts the instrument from her shoulder, she sees him for the first time and smiles, and he wishes that the joy in her look had something to do with him. "There you are," she says. "Sorry I woke you."

He releases his hold on the doorframe and looks at his stinging hands. The wooden corners have bitten bright red furrows into his palms, straight cuts that blot out the subtler pattern of his skin and impose an ugly new design against the grain. Bringing them into focus causes the room beyond them to tilt precariously, perpendicular angles becoming acute, edges gathering shadows as if taking on dusk.

"Hey." Elizabeth starts up from her chair. The bow clatters against the cello, and the instrument's polished recesses resound with a startling depth. "Are you okay?" In two strides she reaches him and places her hand on his shoulder. "It wasn't that bad, was it?"

Kevin shakes his head. "There are worse things to wake up to." He rubs his hands across his blue jeans and looks down at her face. It contains an expression he has never seen before. Beneath the concern and the tightness of her forced smile, he thinks she looks moved. "No," he says. "It wasn't bad at all, actually. I guess I just forgot I was breathing there for a second. You know, people get old, and they can only do one thing at a time."

She attempts to guide him toward the couch, urging him into a sitting position. "Elizabeth, please—" Kevin tries to extricate himself, but he has not yet recovered from the moment of vertigo, and now she is both faster and stronger than he is. They are halfway across the room—how did she get him so far? The sofa cushions press against the back of his knees.

"One minute, Dad. Just give it one minute." She pulls on his elbow, but he continues to resist. "If standing in the living room makes you dizzy, I really hate to think of you up on the edge of—"

"Goddammit, Elizabeth!" He flings her arm away, and she steps back and does not try to touch him again. "There's nothing wrong with me. You don't have to make a big deal out of every little thing."

He takes a tentative step and, sure enough, the world has regained its normal equilibrium, everything solid and steady. He does not turn to look back at her, but as he leaves the room he tries to cast his parting words in a conciliatory tone. "There isn't anything here for breakfast, so I'm going to go to the store—I was thinking omelets. Is that all right with you?"

"Whatever you want," she says, and the stiffness in her response pains him. As he makes his way out the door, keys in hand, he hears her playing resume once again, a roughened and frustrated edge to the notes that was not there before.

The route from his house to the closest grocery store runs almost entirely uphill, bending back around on itself east and then west in deference to the bluffs that overlook the Pacific. Kevin has guided his Toyota around these parabolic curves more times than he can count with just a tilt of his arm on the steering wheel, not a thought in his head. Now, however, something vibrates along his nerve endings like a delayed reaction, possibly a residual effect of his earlier light-headedness that heightens his awareness of physical forces, the power of friction and velocity and speed. The window next to him quivers with every car that hurtles past, metal masses separated by mere inches, there and then gone. He stares at the asphalt churning in front of him, the sleek yellow dashes flowing past, and concentrates on maintaining a constant margin of space.

After half a mile, he has almost gained enough altitude to see over the roofs of the houses that jostle along the beach for the tiniest sliver of a view—a precious blue glint between fences over a three-car garage—to where a narrow strip of sand suns itself below. The light catching and reflecting in his mirrors causes his eyes to smart and water, blurring the scene in front of him, and he brushes them angrily with the backs of his hands, one and then the other.

So that is what he is doing then—that hasty and irritated gesture—when, just above him, a flaming red sports car dips over the crest of the hill and collides headlong into him. He swings his gaze around just in time to see the impact as it occurs: the sky breaking into shards, the red hood wrinkling, a spray of glass and sparks. The centrifugal spin and the airbag exploding out from the steering column drive him back into his seat, and he feels the Toyota slipping out of the vortex into the open space where the ocean shines. The vehicle strikes the guardrail, which resists, bows, tears away with a metallic sound, screws and solder shuddering defeat. He feels the earth slither out from under the rear tires; caught on the edge, the car hangs, wobbles, wavers in a strange equilibrium.

No film could capture all these excruciating, astonishing details, each one faceted with a thousand others: the clouds snagged in the sparkling blue fragments of the passenger window, the parenthetical grass blades fluttering skyward, the filament jutting from a headlight gone blind. A refrain sings through his head, five repeating tones, a piercing iteration so sustained that at first he thinks what he hears is just the sound of the crash ringing on in his ears. But no, it's a fragment of music from just half an hour earlier when he stood in the doorway and watched the early-morning light burn a rim around Elizabeth's head, a phrase he doesn't even remember retaining.

Over and over the notes bear down, rise, then descend again, the pattern breaking off before it resolves. Each time the sequence begins anew Kevin remembers to take a breath. With each inhalation sharp pains radiate outward from his sternum along the fragile branches of his ribs, thousands of microscopic fibers conflagrating in spreading rings like a grass fire. Flames flicker in the gloom behind his eyelids. He opens them. The sun catches in his lashes; he blinks furiously and bright spangles flash and scatter everywhere he looks. Beyond that everything is dark.

But when he turns his head and focuses his dilated pupils,

the other driver resolves slowly in the haze. She's a young woman—about Elizabeth's age—although her pale and unexceptional face in no way resembles his daughter's. And yet the shadows from the interior of her car distill the strange girl's features—the hollows beneath her cheekbones, the flush of her lips, the square angle of her jaw—into something exquisite in its own right. Her head thrusts back against her seat cushion as if she is straining toward a surface for air. Then she opens her eyes; she watches him through the empty space where her windshield existed mere seconds earlier.

The woman stares on and on as if she wants to speak and would if only she could while those notes burrow farther and farther into him, rising in volume, threatening to overwhelm him. He wants to close his eyes again, but he can't bring himself to look away from her. There's something so knowing in the gaze fixed upon him that Kevin wonders if she can't hear it too somehow, that maddening irresolution.

How many times has he found himself on a brink, ready to pass over the edge? Kevin estimates the time of the required motions and the effect of their momentum on the car's sway—the kind of calculations where he holds expertise although it's an imprecise science at best. He thinks he might make it. With his left hand, he flings open the driver's side door; water or maybe sand lies below, but he doesn't spare a glance to find out. With the dead fingers of his right, he fumbles with the clasp on his seat belt. It springs away easily under his touch.

Kevin performs each movement with deliberation and care. Not because he should but because he must—slowly the feeling in his extremities is ebbing away. With each second that passes he is astounded. The Toyota should already be on its way down—it's oscillating in a terrifying pitch—and yet somehow here it stays. He can reach out and grasp a post of the guardrail and, one slow inch at a time, he can pull himself free. The effort forces the blood back where it needs to go, and he feels his fingers and toes again aching along to the same tempo that drums in his head.

This should be painful, and it is, but it isn't so terrible. That's what Kevin wants to tell her, so he lifts himself up and struggles slowly across the pavement and sandy topsoil to the mangled sports car. Jagged teeth of glass still hang in the driver's window making it difficult to fit his hand in, but with a bit of effort he reaches through, brushes his palm across the young woman's clammy forehead, and pats her damp hair while she closes her eyes and sits very still, waiting. From where he stands, just back behind the edge, the view is astonishing: the effusive air, grains of sand taking flight in the wind, the water stretching for miles.

Now that he's here, he can't think of how to ask the question or to describe what he knows. It isn't what he expected, it's not the way anyone else guessed, *flashing* not right, not even coming close, but rather each second of his life unfurling at once. It's as if the ocean's every brief and fluid fold—every blazing peak and shaded trough—has paused before him, and somehow he can see each of them, now one at a time, now too many to count, all merging together in startling glitters of light. Strangers gather somewhere in the background, and all his words are failing him, dying soundless and insufficient on his dry lips. So Kevin offers her the first sounds that come to him. "Shh, shh," he says. "There, there."

BLACKOUT

I T'S A LITTLE AFTER six in the morning when Paul calls
from Alaska to tell me he has arrived. Three takeoffs,
three landings, a seventy-three-mile trek in a Jeep with no
shocks, and one flat tire north of Noatak, but he has made it.
I am standing in the middle of our living room drinking my
second cup of coffee. "How's the light?" I ask. He is speaking
to me on the satellite phone that the magazine gave him,
and in addition to the tinny edge it gives his voice, there is a
strange muttering sound in the background, like someone
mumbling in a low and tremulous register.

"Unearthly," he says. "Even at one in the morning. The
sky is—there it goes—it's pulsing."

A small burst of static sizzles in my ear, and while I
wait for it to subside I step in and out of my shoes,
complicated one-two footwork on the hardwood. Through
the second-story window, anchorless tree branches waft
up and down in the heat, and out on the street two car

horns perform a brief and dissonant duet. "Are you there?" Paul asks.

"Of course."

"I said, I've heard one of the physiological effects of severe jetlag is a tendency to see auras."

"Right." I look up and glance at the rectangular numbers above the stove. "Way to kill the mystery."

"I was just—"

"I know, I know. We're just getting going here, though. I have to roust Leah."

In fact, Leah does not need rousting. When I knock lightly on her door and push it open, she is sprawled on the purple rag rug at the foot of her rumpled bed reading a book, one bare leg kicked out, the other bent. I cannot see the scuffed cover of the paperback behind it. It's probably the dictionary. Regardless of her surroundings, she always sits like that, as if she has been dropped and cannot remember how to realign her elbows or knees. My heart skips for one moment as I glimpse the striped bruising across her lean shins, but then I realize, no, it's simply a quirk of the light, the violet braids in the rug refracting around her limbs, nothing more. I cross the room and tug apart the thin curtains, and Leah lifts the book to shield her face. It is the dictionary. I can see the bolded words, their syllables strung between the black typeset beads, staggered across the pages. The Ds.

"Did you sleep okay?"

"So-so." She lifts her hand and tips it from side to side. "Dad made it, I take it."

"He did. Will you be ready to go in a few minutes?"

"I've been ready to go for hours." She drops her head back to her book and resumes her reading, jiggling her foot with concentration. I step out, carefully cracking the door behind me, and set off down the hall to seek out our deaf old collie. Ansel has turned restless in his advanced age, sleeping every night in a new nook, behind a new chair, and now our morning ritual contains this little game of hide-and-seek. No matter how carefully Leah or I bend down and stroke his ear he lurches to his feet, wide-eyed, splayed-legged, astounded to have come out of the dark.

Hours, I think, as I stand on the porch, watching Ansel drift across our tiny patch of front lawn, scrounging vaguely for a whiff of anything he hasn't smelled the day before. Hours is probably not an exaggeration. Leah is always awake—even at the odd times I get off my shifts. At midnight, at seven in the morning. None of the books I bought three years ago when she turned twelve said anything about this. If anything, they'd said the exact opposite. *The long durations the typical adolescent spends in bed can often strike adults as excessive—a symptom of laziness.* I'd hidden the books under my nightstand knowing Paul would make fun of them. When he finally found one, he did. "What are you reading these things for, Denise?" he had said. "It's not like she's going to grow another head."

"I just want a bit of forewarning," I replied defensively. "To hear some people talk, that's exactly what happens."

"Some people are idiots," Paul said.

At last, Ansel squats arthritically in the grass, and I impatiently tap my knuckles on the railing. "Attaboy, Ansel," I say out of habit, although he won't hear me. I have to spring down the steps and take him by the collar. It hasn't rained in over two weeks, and all the grass has a scourged look to it. You can see straight through the dry tangles to the packed dirt, where small stones have surfaced and are sunning their glittering hides in the sun.

Ansel's back is covered in whorls like the map of a storm system. He would stay outside all day if I let him, stalking the evil wasps until he dropped over dead from the heat. We're both unsteady on our feet this morning. I have to boost his back end up the stairs; in doing so I stumble twice, and the second time I go down. When we finally reach the top, Leah is standing behind the screen door watching our sad two-ring circus and tapping her brown lunch bag against her knee. I don't know how much she's seen.

"I'm off," she says.

"All right, then." She is now taller than I am, and I have to stand on my tiptoes to kiss her forehead. There's an ascetic severity to the centered white part that curves over the crown of her head. It makes her look like a Quaker, imposes a kind of piety on her thin and serious face. "Remember I'm working a double shift today, so I won't be home until late."

I watch her turn out of the gate and down the crooked sidewalk, off into the world. She drags her feet as she walks, stares dutifully straight ahead. The sun beating down on her is so intense that before she's gone a block, small dark curves have blossomed through the back of her thin blue cotton T-shirt, just below her shoulder blades, like wings.

Our house is about two miles from the hospital where I work. I can take the bus, but I prefer to walk on all but the most inclement of days, to set my feet in motion and fall into the meditative state that repetition inspires. The majority of my route takes me through neighborhoods like our own—rows of old townhouses on rippling streets. Each narrow house has been cobbled onto the one before it like an afterthought, constructed on architectural inclinations all its own, and the result—little switchback staircases, a corner bowed in concession to the ancient trunk of an elm, a shade garden beneath a wrought-iron grate—is one of pleasing idiosyncrasy. Daisies spill across the gates; some of them have insinuated themselves between the mismatched concrete rectangles of the sidewalk, which have begun to list and separate with the years.

Not far from the hospital, however, the blocks take on a seedier quality, the houses more shambling, the flowers growing scant, until I cross into a—park is not quite the word for it. It's a small scrap of land owned by the city, but no one has done any upkeep on it for years. Long weeds trail across the path; crumpled cans glint from the depths of them and plastic bags balloon from their fringed ends, swelling and shrinking with the breeze. Today they stir only slightly like faint breathing; the air is so still.

In the center of this wild patch a few homeless people sleep on the scarred planks of benches around a neglected fountain. The tarnished silver water in its stone basin reflects a dim variation of the sky. The state of homelessness is typically a transient one; most who fall into it are out on the street for less than a week, but here in this park are the veterans—I have seen them for years and know them by sight. A man whose pachydermatous feet strain at the unfastened straps of his sandals. An old woman with pale eyes so clouded by cataracts that her gaze is as opaque and swirled as an atmosphere; she is lost beneath it. I pass and nod to her, but she simply rocks to herself and does not see me.

As the hospital looms before me, I glance down and check my watch. Leah should be at the school by now. The thought of her sitting down at a desk so early in the morning on a day when most high school students across the city are still sleeping, readying themselves for a day at the beach or the movie theater makes me sigh out loud. Two months ago, when the nuns at Leah's school had urged this upon us, this summer program for "gifted and challenging students," Paul had been ambivalent. "I don't trust anything buried under those kind of euphemisms," he said when I told him about it. "There's always a stink at the bottom."

But my conference with Leah's teacher had frightened me. The woman and I had faced each other across a bare wooden tabletop in one of the empty classrooms. There was nothing between us except a single stark line of reflected light. Sister Clarence set her elbows down and folded her hands along it. "I'm going to be frank with you," she'd said. "I think there is something wrong with your daughter."

I had been staring down at the woman's neatly coiled fists, but I looked up when she said this. The immense glasses she wore bowed her face out at the edges and imbued her eyes with excessive detail. When we'd enrolled Leah in Catholic school, I'd had a ridiculous romantic vision of habits and rosaries, but the sister was adorned with nothing more ornamental than a blue skirt and collared shirt buttoned all the way to her neck. "She gets beautiful grades," I said. "I know she is very tightly wrapped. Maybe a bit too interiorized."

"She never says anything." Sister Clarence leaned forward in her chair. "I'm not being hyperbolic here, Mrs. Fletcher. I have been keeping notes for the past few months. Not a word in class and not to any of her classmates—which of course always concerns us more."

"She talks." My voice sounded shrill even to my own ears. "She may not have many friends, but that doesn't mean something is wrong with her. Just because she's not one of those girls who's always flapping her—"

"There's no need to be defensive." Sister Clarence did not blink an eye. "We're both on the same side. You must remember, though, that sometimes people who are at a distance can see things more clearly. We have a moral obligation to speak the truth when something important is at stake. And I'm telling you now. This is not normal."

The hospital where I work was built about a hundred years ago, completed not long before the outbreak of the First World War. It's a dour catacomb of a place with slitted windows and thick brick walls that always feel dank to the touch. I have a difficult time imagining the consumptive crowds that were once nursed here doing anything other than dying like flies. After a philanthropic windfall in the early nineties, an enormous new wing was added, a blinding glass-and-steel tower that looms above the surrounding neighborhoods. The old wing was taken over by the nearby medical school and converted into classrooms and a collection of small cell-like labs and the patient beds were whisked away from the gloom and sibilant radiators and into the pristine hushed halls, partitioned off by doors that whisked open and closed at the touch of a button, and sealed off pockets of antiseptic air in their wake. Our transplant center is nationally recognized. At all hours of the day and night, helicopters carrying hearts, livers, and corneas land and take off from the roof above our heads. So well-soundproofed are the walls around us that unless you are listening for them—that far-off stuttering—you cannot hear them coming or going.

In a place so insulated from the world, illuminated always in a surreal state of permaday, the hours have a strange fluidity to them. The shadows are fixed at right angles under the fluorescent lighting, never shifting, except across the curtains of the shaded nooks where the sleeping stir. These patients on the eighth floor, where I work—the transplant patients—have undergone the most invasive surgical procedures yet developed by modern science—operations that take eight to fourteen hours, equipment that costs millions of dollars, precise handiwork that takes surgeons years to acquire. The first time I observed one of these spectacles as a nursing student, I was dazzled by its complexity. The intricate order of steps, the exactness of the incisions, the subtle give-and-take of the gestures—all on the gaping, ever-shifting terrain of a body, no two ever the same.

And yet lately, I am struck by the crudeness of the work. There's such an element of butchery to it—carving out a piece of a person and replacing it with a stranger's, hoping it takes. The people who make it out look ravaged—held together by stitching, bruised in spectacular colors, swollen beyond recognition. A few months ago, I stopped assisting in those desperate marathon procedures. Over time I have begun to prefer the soothing tasks of working the floor—taking temperatures, administering medication, keeping an eye on the machines that monitor a patient's tenuous connection to life.

I rarely work double shifts anymore, especially while Paul is away. The one I took today a last-minute favor to a nurse named Bette, who had to leave town suddenly to be with her ill mother. I have forgotten how hard it is to stand all day, to walk quietly, to hold my head up and stay aware. At ten o'clock in the evening, with one hour left on my shift, I climb the ten floors to the roof. I have not taken a break since lunch.

Stepping outside is like pressing your face into a body, warm and damp to the point of suffocating. Nurses and techs cluster around the perimeter of the building, smoking and talking quietly. The majority of the nurses smoke. The doctors, with few exceptions, do not. A liver is scheduled to arrive shortly, so the floodlights around the landing pad have been switched on, and everyone's features are cast in a dramatic chiaroscuro—all hooded eyes and flickering fingers that spin and twine the smoke. Most of them are looking up, straining their eyes toward the dimming sky. The techs collect a small pool—the first person to spot the Survival Flight chopper claims a free lunch in the cafeteria the next day. I never win this game and do not play it.

Instead I turn and stare out over the railing at the glittering constellation of the city at my feet, small stars blinking on and shutting off, headlights streaking across their orbits, one after another. From across the roof, a shout goes up, "Thar she blows!" and then a smattering of applause and boos. Because everyone else is straining their gaze upward, I am the first person to see the city go dark—a blackening that starts on the horizon and races toward us—an orderly but breathtakingly swift advance like knitting unraveling—and before I can even exclaim it has engulfed us. The building shudders and dims, and then the generators beneath us kick to life with an audible jolt. The very air smells of electricity.

"Clear the deck!" someone yells, and then the helicopter is overhead with its thought-obliterating roar, churning the stagnant air into a frenzy, whipping the parallel lines of shadow and light into a series of tangled snapping ends. On cue, everyone takes off running, straining through the wind like water, scrubs billowing, hair bristling like tentacles, all charged with purpose, animated again, all trying to think and breathe at once.

When I board the southbound bus, an hour later, the electricity is still not back on. Traffic is backed up along all the major streets; each intersection beneath its dark and gutted traffic light must be hazarded with a series of nods and hand gestures. Some drivers cautiously bide their time; others blaze through with one hand on the horn. The police, clad in reflective green vests are out at the worst of them, flailing their arms in the headlights as if they are trying to wave down planes.

Our bus driver is a grizzled old man with an expression of beatific patience. He depresses and releases the brake pedal as if nothing whatsoever were amiss with the world. Around me, the other passengers stare grimly at their own reflections in the glass.

Someone in the back calls for the radio to be turned up. The power is out all along the Eastern Seaboard, as far south as Richmond and far north as Boston. No one knows exactly why yet, but it appears there has been a massive grid failure. The radio announcer is interviewing an electrical engineer who talks at great length about the energy-sucking greed of air-conditioners. There is nothing more specific to blame at this juncture, but I know that will come. Except for the sound of idling engines, the night is eerily quiet. The blackness presses against the windows and each flash of passing headlights illuminates the pale whorls of fingerprints, hundreds of them as if someone had tried to climb the pane. Then they vanish into the darkness again.

Leah is lying on the couch reading a book when I walk through the door. A bowl, its bottom crusted with the splinters of potato chips, sits on the floor beside her elbow. Next to that a white taper leans at a precarious angle from a coffee mug. The wax beads are slipping along the candle and pooling on the lip of the mug, threatening a downward advance to the rug.

"Ugh," I say to the guttering light. "How can you see anything?"

"It's not that bad." She turns the page.

"Well." I carefully shake off my shoes and sink to the floor behind the couch. "I'm afraid we might be in for the long haul here, kiddo." There's a loose scrap of paper with Leah's handwriting resting along the baseboard, and I pick it up and turn it over in my hand. As I stare at it thoughtlessly, I remember the morning after my meeting with Sister Clarence, how I had found Leah's homework on the kitchen table, a paper full of diagrammed sentences, their clauses spreading out, participle from gerund, like the branching of a tree. I had believed diagramming sentences to be a lost art, but there it was. The beautifully even curves of her penmanship had caused my throat to tighten. Surely, I thought, a person who could execute what was required of her with such grace—surely she would find her way in the world. I crease the paper carefully and slip it in my pocket. "How was class?" I ask her.

"It was fine." One sock-clad foot twitches above the back of the couch. "Tolerable."

"Succinctly put, as always."

"We read some poetry."

"Anything good?"

"Some Frost. Some Cummings. I've read it before."

"Well, la-dee-dah." I say the words as gently as I can. She

cannot see my face, and she will not assume that I am teasing her. "Did you have any interesting conversations?"

The foot twitches and disappears back into the depths of the couch. She mutters something inaudible.

"I can't hear you, Leah. You need to enunciate. Remember what Sister Clarence said?"

"I said." She sits up and stares at me over the cushions. Even in the flickering light I can see the places where she has been picking at her skin, pink patches on her cheeks and chin, as though she's been stung. Her shining eyes are startlingly fierce, and my stomach drops at the sight of their sudden level gaze. "No one ever tells me the truth anymore."

Paul is not answering his phone. I check my watch and perform the brief subtraction in my head—at twelve o'clock in the morning, this math requires more effort than it should. Eight o'clock. My husband is roaming the tundra at the top of the world, photographing the Inupiat or walruses on glaciers that are melting into the sea. Now that they are going, everyone wants pictures. I pace the dark halls, and every time I enter a room, flick the light switch before I remember. Every window in the house is pressed tightly shut, but the muggy outside air is slowly stealing in around us through the ventilation shafts. I can feel it. Almost all of my neighbors have bedded down for the night—the white scribbling of flashlight beams in the dark windows has vanished.

Feeling my way with my feet, I descend down into the black depths of the bottom floor of our townhouse. The door of the little laundry room beneath our stairs is shut tightly, and the only way I can make this out is to brush its grooved surface with my hands. Paul still uses this space as a darkroom—the walls exhale an astringent chemical stench—but very rarely because now he has a gleaming new camera that instantly captures his pictures on a tiny intricate screen—no need for film or fixing solutions or waiting in the dark. The grunt work eliminated by this technology is his and not my own, so I have never asked him if anything else might be lost—no more carrying the silvery germs of unknown possibilities with you through strange cities and across unknown terrains, submerging them, hoping for something lovely to swim up from the depths. I admit that I find it depressing—the universe reduced to an arrangement of pixels. I alluded to this once, and Paul ruffled my hair, and said, "Sure, but the end result is the same, is it not?"

The burst of the phone, one floor above me, through the still house, is electrifying. For a minute I flounder as if I have been dropped into deep water; I cannot find the stairs. But then I regain my footing and make it to the kitchen before the final ring.

"Hey," Paul says. Sometimes he sounds startled when I answer the phone at my own house, as if he expected another woman to pick up. "You called from the landline. I almost didn't recognize the number."

"I did," I say. "The power is out. Our other phones aren't working."

"Mm." This news does not interest him in the least, and he cannot pretend otherwise. "I thought maybe something was wrong."

"Well," I say, but then somehow I do not know quite what it was I meant to tell him. "I mean, no, nothing apart from the usual. How are things up there?"

"Extraordinary." He speaks like this whenever he is out on a shoot, prone to using superlatives, his voice slightly winded. "We're sleeping in tents, and you can see the borealis right through the walls. The birds sing until midnight. It's amazing."

"That must make it difficult to sleep." I'm surprised by the edge to my voice, but the subtleties of inflection are lost in the transmission, and Paul does not make them out. He talks on, telling me how they take the boys out hunting, boys younger than Leah, the bloodiness of the killing, but I am having a difficult time hearing him over that strange low mumbling noise. It's louder than before, or maybe I am simply too tired to pick and choose what I hear, and all the sounds are merging together.

"Paul." I have to interrupt him at last. "I worked a double shift. I can't think straight. I'll call you later." And we say good-bye.

The alarm on my wristwatch wakes me the next morning. This mess we're caught in has still not been resolved—I understand this even before I roll over and catch sight of the blank face on my bedside clock. The air around me has a deadened feel to it—none of the reassuring clicks of air being compressed, of currents humming through the wires. Ansel, for once, is awake before me, and he regards me anxiously, his chin on the mattress. I am stuck to my sheets, and when I peel myself away, I can see the creases they have impressed upon me during the dreamless night, like the rivers in an atlas.

I am not due at the hospital until noon, but I have to send Leah off. The woman who answers the phone at St. Thomas informs me that yes, they have a generator. The school is still open today, so while Leah brushes her teeth upstairs, I patch together a peanut butter sandwich and wrap a bunch of grapes in plastic. The fruit in the bowl on the counter is ripening too quickly—a few forerunner flies are already scouting out the tawny horizons of our apples. I do not open the refrigerator.

Leah appears silently at the foot of the stairs. It is as if she has lost weight in the night—there's something birdlike about the bones in her wrists, a sharpened delicacy in the cleft at the base of her throat. She's turning translucent around the edges. What will I feed her? I wonder. We cannot subsist for days on end on peanut butter, and everything in the kitchen is going soft and sour.

Ansel trails at her heels, and as she passes through the door, he makes an unexpected dash after her. I barely catch his collar as the screen door recoils, and the moment he has been safely snagged, I stare down at him, dumbfounded. I cannot remember the last time I saw him move with such speed. Out loud, to Leah's retreating back, I say, "You make quite a pair, Ansel." My silent daughter, my deaf dog.

I leave for work early. Even in the bright morning sunlight, the windows in the houses appear strangely opaque. I cannot remember the last time I have seen the city so quiet. All the side streets have been transformed into wide and spacious avenues. The occasional car rolls cautiously past, its driver unable to quite believe it—all that pavement and no need to share it with anyone. Even the homeless in the park have disappeared. Their benches are empty, and the pale decrees carved in the dark green painted slats blaze like runes in the morning light. Still, the afterimages of those mysterious equations linger on my retinas; shining imprints that hang between me and the rest of the world. There's a photographic trick that creates this effect. Paul explained it to me once, how you burn one negative after another onto the same paper. No matter how well you do it though, he said to me, the merging is never completely seamless. If you care enough, if you know where to look, you can find the sutures, the small discrepancies in clarity and proportion, in lighting and shadow that give away the lie.

When the doors of the emergency room part around me, I am dazzled. It's startling, this pristine vista full of hard surfaces all sparkling before my eyes. I have been in the unmitigated heat and the silence for so many hours that the hum of the refrigerated air around me gives me vertigo. I have to slump into the plastic chair nearest to me and put my head between my knees. It suddenly occurs to me that I have not eaten since lunch the day before. And I think, so at least this makes sense. Blue tiles beneath my feet blur and then come into focus again.

The man sitting next to me smells like he has been pickled

in gin. I did a few rotations in the ER as an intern, and we used to try to guess the blood-alcohol levels of the drunks that came in before their tests were run. I got pretty good at it. Going by my nose, I'd put this man at a 0.2. He puts his hand on my back and rubs it kindly. It's hard for me to understand the words he speaks to me. They're missing so many consonants, but I think he says, "Just give it time."

"Denise." It's Nancy, calling at me from behind the desk. "Are you all right over there?"

I open my eyes. The floor tiles are clear once again, an orderly expanse of squares stretching out in all directions, rows and columns marred only here and there by a black comma of shoe scuff. I straighten cautiously in my seat.

"Does she look all right to you?" My drunken neighbor has taken up my cause, and it would be almost funny, except it isn't. "She is not all right. Get this woman a doctor. Get her a priest."

"I'm fine." I push to my feet and sling my bag over my shoulder. It's heavy, as if I have packed stones. Nancy rolls her eyes at me as I trudge by her.

"Did you hear the radio?" she asks. "*Days*, Denise. Days. That's what they're saying. We're just supposed to live like this."

I start to answer, but I'm distracted by the sight of an elderly woman in a wheelchair sitting by herself near the double doors. She's wrapped in a cotton robe covered in fading starfish. With the light streaming in behind her, I can see straight through it to the outline of her emaciated limbs, entwined in the clear tubing of her oxygen tank. The wild white wisps of her hair shine. She's watching me; when she sees me looking back she smiles to herself and turns away. So sly and knowing is her expression that I do not see right away the flicker between her knotted hands. I am slow, caught in suspension, waiting to understand, and when I do I drop my bag and lunge toward her, calling out, so that everyone in the waiting room turns just in time to see the woman bring the cigarette to her lips and burst spectacularly into flames.

"That's horrifying," Paul says. Through the bedroom window, the city has begun its fade into black beneath the purple sky, and darkness is rising like a tide in the empty streets. Already, I can no longer see my bare feet; in another fifteen minutes my legs will be gone entirely.

"Yes," I say. "That's the word." For a moment we are quiet together, and I listen to the low sobbing chant on the line between us. "You really can't hear that?" I say at last. "It sounds like Latin, you know, like choral singing."

"It isn't on my end," Paul says. He sounds impatient. "It must be a transmission problem on your side."

The walls of our bedroom, like the rest of our house, are covered with Paul's pictures. They're still discernible in the creeping dusk—sleek rectangular landscapes shot with slow shutter speeds, so everything in them is blurred and rippling. There's something desolate about them, time stretched out so long that the people in them are nothing more than ghostly smears across a moonscape pavement; the glass bottles and manhole covers glint as sharp and clear as archaeological finds. I say, "I don't know about that."

Paul clears his throat. The sound of it, projected with abrupt clarity, hurts my chest. "So obviously it *wasn't* the right word, then. I'm sorry. I'm sorry, Denise. I don't know what you want me to say."

"It's not—I just—" I'm staring at the picture of Leah hanging above our bed. Paul took it the autumn she was three. She is sitting in a pile of leaves, almost buried beneath them, and her arms are thrown up toward the yellow leaves streaked above her like sunbeams. The joy in the moment is utterly without effort. "I just can't shake this sense that I'm a beat behind. It's like I faltered somewhere back, and now I can't quite regain my—"

The phone is guttering in and out, emanating strange sizzles and wavering pitches like a dying star, but I can still make out his voice. He says, "What is it you want from me?"

"I want you to come home." I do not know I am going to say the words until I have said them.

And then it's quiet, so quiet that I can hear his steady breathing as if he's in the room with me. He says, "I can't."

After we hang up the phone I sit carefully down at the foot of the bed and watch the mosaic of violet sky trembling in the leaves of the tree outside my window. The bedroom door stands closed between my back and the hallway, but I can hear Leah in the kitchen opening and closing drawers, searching for something in the dark. In the stillness, the sound of even the subtlest gesture flows without resistance through the walls and open windows. The scraping of fork tines across a plate. The scuffing of sock feet thumping lazily down the stairs. The rhythmic creaking of a bed on hardwood. Two streams of breath merging and then coming apart again. I do not make a move. What will keep them from hearing me?

When I finally collect myself and make my way downstairs, Leah is in front of the open fridge, peering into its dim warm depths, not doing anything else, just staring. She's standing on one leg, one foot resting on her knee like a crane. An earthy scent wafts up around her in the muggy air of the kitchen. I can just make out the neglected plate of food I brought her from the hospital cafeteria—broccoli and two baked potatoes—at her feet. Ansel hunches over it furtively, licking the buttered insides out of the split potato skins with tender strokes of his tongue.

"Look," she says, and I enter the kitchen and stand beside her. There's the dough I made before Paul left for Alaska, before the heat made the idea of baking awful. Over the past two days in the warmth and the darkness, the yeast has budded in on itself over and over, swelling out of its dish and folding itself around the vegetables and glass jars. The ballooning growth is pale in the way things are that never see the sun—and strangely phosphorescent like mushrooms in a cave.

Leah reaches out her hand and presses it flat against the swell spilling over the top shelf. When she lifts it, the dough rises slowly again, the imprint of her fingers undoing itself. We are both a little mesmerized. It will keep growing, I think. I do not know how we will make it stop.

"What are we going to do?" Leah asks at last. Maybe she's having visions of the downstairs being overrun, this pallid monstrosity engulfing everything in its path. I am seeing it too. I know it's ridiculous, but all this time in the dark—it is doing something to us. Every possibility suddenly looms like a large and open-ended question that cannot be ignored.

I lean on the refrigerator door and consider. Leah bends over the counter, chin in one hand, and swings from side to side on her elbow, watching me.

We end up drowning it. This process requires more work than I anticipated—the dough has spread down the back and sides of the refrigerator, infiltrating the cracks running along the tongue-and-groove shelving. I scrape away at it with my fingernails. Leah stands behind me and holds a flashlight over my head. Every few minutes or so the beam begins to dim—she rattles it, and the light, resuscitated, comes back again. Sweat rises across my back with the effort of scratching and pummeling, my beating fists sink ineffectually down into the white billows and come back smelling like something sour. Again and again my thoughts begin to steal away from me, descending into dark thickets. Again and again I call them back and ask Leah to lift the flashlight higher. I cannot remember why I chose to begin this undertaking now, when it will be most difficult, but I have to finish what I have started. Ansel has given up on us and fallen asleep in the corner of the kitchen. Every now and then I can hear his bony limbs shift on the tile and then fall silent again. We have lit the gas burner on the stove with a match, and the blue iris flickers beneath the teakettle.

When I am finished, when I have torn away all the soft tendrils and finished pounding the overgrown mess back into the tin it grew out of, it is as heavy in my hands as a brick. I drop it into the sink and the instant the boiling water hits it, the yeast plumes upward, rushing toward the steaming surface, white wraiths falling short and dissolving. "Look at that," Leah says. She sounds almost melancholy.

Someone across the street has lit a bonfire. Our walls leap up and fall away, and every now and then a photographed face flashes briefly at us, some stranger's eyes, the plane of a cheek turning away, a jaw set with some troubling thought that Paul managed to catch at the moment it surfaced. I was pregnant with Leah when we moved into this house and not allowed to lift anything heavy, but I spent days arranging my husband's pictures on the walls, trying to decide how best to carve away all the blank space around me—all those wide expanses and little niches. When I was finished I walked through the rooms and realized I was surrounded by people I did not know. Paul has a gift, I am told, an unerring sense for the heart of things, an intuition about those moments upon which everything hinges. I looked at his photographs, and I knew it was true, and I wanted to understand, but when I asked him about it, he scratched his chin and said that it was something he couldn't explain to me—an instinct, an act without thought and ruined by talking.

I thought that time would accustom me to the faces, that some consideration would give them familiarity and meaning, but this has not been the case. There was a night last fall when Paul was in Mongolia, and I couldn't sleep. I walked through the downstairs lifting the pictures from the hooks and turning them to face the wall. I thought Leah was sleeping, but she was not. I was reaching up over the sofa when I heard her footsteps on the stairs. I had a wide oak frame in my hands; as I turned to face her it slipped between my fingers. "What are you doing?" she said to me, and I only barely managed to catch it, to keep it from crashing to the floor where it surely would have shattered: frame, glass, lovely shadowed image, loosed, cartwheeling away from me.

Leah covers the top of the flashlight and rattles it again. "Ta-da." She holds it out to me like a card trick. Her hand is glowing, pink webbing between the dense gray shafting of her metacarpals—proximal, distal—I used to know the names of all those tiny bones. I have forgotten most of them now.

Someone out on the street smashes a bottle. I can hear the glass ringing and scattering over the pavement. The voices of our neighbors swell in its wake, but still all the words remain indistinct.

Next to me Leah shifts and sighs. "This is all completely useless," she says. She lifts the flashlight above her head and rattles it with both hands. The batteries clatter inside the plastic casing like the flat percussions of a primitive instrument. "If I were on a sinking boat and I had to signal through the fog for someone to come get me, this piece of crap would never cut it. How the hell would I be saved?"

She drops her hand; for a second I am blinded. The

dark room rushes away from me in a flash, and I wave at her helplessly.

"Leah."

"Sorry." The beam swings away and goes out. I press my hands to my eyes, cumbersome organs, always trying to keep out light when they should be letting it in, or the other way around.

After a moment, she says, "You didn't answer my question." She walks to the window and leans her elbows on the sill. "And don't say that you'd come for me. You're a terrible swimmer. I've seen you."

I have nearly reached her, but at this I draw back my hand and rest it on my sticky collarbone instead. "Thank you," I say. I grind my fingers into the notch of my clavicle. The bone pushes back. "Thank you very much."

She glances back over her shoulder at me and then begins nervously twisting a strand of hair around her finger. "I only meant . . ." She lets the thought die.

"It was pretty clear." I glance at the face of my watch as if I can read the numbers. *We have a moral obligation to speak the truth.* Those nuns worrying about my daughter, and the whole time she'd been taking their words straight to heart. I'm being too sensitive, but I can't help it. I am stinging as if I have just been slapped. "It's getting pretty late, Leah. It might be a good idea for you to think about hitting the sack."

"Think, think, think." Leah picks up the flashlight and smacks it down onto the windowsill. A sound of plastic cracking. She looks up at me; her lips are white. "There," she says. There is satisfaction in her voice. "Now I've ruined it." And with that she marches into the dark. She steps emphatically on each stair, every footfall meant to be heard.

I sleep through my alarm and when I open my eyes, the room is bright with late morning. I have slept on top of the covers with the phone, which I must have left on the bed after my conversation with Paul. The cord is tangled around my elbow; this is an awful way to start the day, trying to extricate yourself from the elaborate knots that sleep has tightened. The phone has left a crescent bruise on my ribs, and I can't understand how I never felt it.

Leah's door is half-open. She is gone. Class would have started an hour ago. The quilt is pulled smooth across the bed, the pillows arranged contritely. I am going to be late to work if I do not move quickly, but I stand there in the doorway, staring at the made bed, an orderly mirage above the disarray of the floor, shorts and T-shirts shed like peeled skins, uneven plateaus of books, some of them buckling, in the middle of a glacial descent. The lavender paint of the walls is almost entirely unadorned except for a scalloped shelf bowing under the weight of a crooked jade plant and a glossy black-and-white portrait of some Victorian writer—probably torn from a book—which has been taped over her bed. The woman's dark hair is looped demurely around her head, but her expression verges on pained. Why Leah chose to place her there, what in that face she wishes to be reminded of, I do not know. Through her narrow window, you can see over the street into the neighbor's yard. From this vantage point, it's glaringly apparent how close they came to loosing disaster upon us—the wide swath of grass singed from the dirt, the roses next to their porch stairs still curling away from the memory of the heat, the elm dropping charred leaves. A bus hurtles by, and all the gray ash rises in its wake.

I arrive at the hospital half an hour late and winded. I jogged the second mile; a dark blue patchwork of sweat has bled through my scrubs, and I pluck the damp fabric off my chest as I wend my way up the gloomy stairwell. One of the cardiologists nods as she passes me on the way down. Her blond hair is bundled messily on top of her head. We're all looking a little worse for the wear. "Today is the day," she says to me, but it's like another language. I don't hear the sentence until we have passed, and even then I can't comprehend its import.

When I reach the eighth floor, Eileen, the shift manager, waves at me from behind the desk. "You're late," she says. Someone calls a code blue, and several people race past. They dodge and weave down the hall, superior in their purpose. "Check on eight two four. Bette hasn't had time."

Room 824 is a heart transplant. A twenty-five-year-old woman who was operated on two days ago. She is sleeping and alone, but there is a chair pushed away from her bed as if someone has just stood up from it, wandered away to find a cup of coffee or to look out a window and search the blank sky for some kind of sign, or to flee the beeping of the monitor. I stand at the end of the bed and flip through her chart. This is her second transplant. The last heart failed her after sixteen months. The transcription will tell me the specific details, but I already know—someone so young hasn't had time yet to wear out her heart; there was something wrong from the very beginning. Maybe they knew it right from the start, or maybe it stayed hidden for years, like a secret. She has a generous face—you can tell even though she's frowning in her sleep—and the long sturdy fingers of a pianist, maybe a bassoon player.

Her temperature is elevated. Nothing too alarming, but it's still inauspicious. I carefully lift her hand, and she stirs, troubled by my touch. Her graceful fingers weigh nothing, and they are cold as snow.

"Emily." I rub her knuckles. I brush back her hair and whisper into her ear, "Emily, can you open your eyes for me?" The monitor beside the bed catches a beat and then picks up speed. A small red petal blossoms on the pale fabric covering her chest, then another one, then another. It won't be long now. I'm holding a roll of gauze; it unravels and races across the floor as I fumble with the button over the bed, keep grinding it down as if that will slow down the seconds or make the call more insistent. Years ago, I knew a girl who said Hail Marys every time she heard an ambulance; she'd drop her head and mutter soundlessly while the sirens raged past. I asked Leah once if she'd ever heard of such a thing, and she said no and looked away.

But now would be a good time to have something to say, moments like these when there are no other niceties. Everything will need to be ready when the room is swarmed, but I am waiting as long as possible to loosen her gown; it's so cold in this stark place, it seems cruel to bare her small chest a second before I have to. I lean over her, one hand on her forehead as if I can expel the warmth of my body into hers, as if the source of those crimson spatters, coming faster now, pooling up, is somewhere above us and I can shield her from the rain. And I stay there even as the footfalls come thundering down the hall, even as they charge through the door and jerk back the curtain, even as they descend upon her.

The ensuing surgery takes forty-five minutes, and in the end they lose her anyway. The chair at the bedside has not been pushed back by the girl's mother, as I imagined, but her boyfriend—a thin young man with loping strides who rounds the corner just as they are wheeling her out. He drops his coffee. The scalding fluid bursts across the floor, and the doctors are yelling at him to get out of the way, get out of the way. "Oh, Emily," he says, but nothing stops and the bed, the doctors, vanish in a silver flash between two swinging doors. We stare at each other in the sudden silence, waiting, but there is nothing else. I have blood on the cuffs of both my sleeves.

I am standing in the locker room, scrubbing at my wrists, one then the other, wringing the gray thermal, sopping to the elbows, when Eileen brings me the news. Pulmonary embolism. And not until they'd opened her up had they discovered the infection. "Her body didn't want that heart. You know sometimes they don't, and that is the way it is."

That's what she says. As if it's some kind of consolation. I hear the words, but I don't look up.

"That is the way it is," I echo her mindlessly. Water chirps in the basin. She's still there standing in the mirror behind me, leaning on one of the lockers and twirling the combination slowly between her fingers. The white numbers revolve around, but the lock will not come undone.

"You didn't bring a change of clothes?"

"I did." I stare back down at the sink and dab at my cuffs again. The blood has almost rinsed away entirely—there is only a jagged trail around each hem like a coastline washing away. "I mean I usually do. I left my bag at home today, that's all."

I straighten up and reach for the paper towels.

"Dave said you looked like you were having a hard time in there."

"No harder than usual." I concentrate on scrubbing my right sleeve, roughing up the tiny gray threads. They will never smooth back down again.

"Denise."

"What?" I think then that I have an inkling how Leah must feel, everyone around her always demanding something from her that she doesn't want to give them.

"Sherry's coming in. She wants to pick up an extra shift. That means I can let someone go. Today it's going to be you. You're the lucky one."

Outside the sky burns without color. There's a breeze picking up, though. Papers swirl past, pale sheets laden with letters and words, sections and subsections, as if someone has been hurling legal documents from a balcony into the wind. I pass a gas station. Its windows are dark, and the handles on the pumps have been tied with yellow tape. NO, says the sign in the window. STOP ASKING. Outside a corner store a raggedy man is selling cans of soup for five dollars apiece. He calls out to me, and keeps calling although I do not turn my head.

It's not a clear thought in my head at first, only a vague impulse, but as I am borne along, I understand that I am going to get my daughter. We'll take the afternoon that has been given to us and drive to the shore or wherever she would like to go. St. Thomas isn't far, and it feels like I'm moving fast, as if the street is flowing under my feet without effort.

St. Thomas is dark—but of course—what did I expect? The building sits on a prim lawn and its brassy facade is wrought with pietas and weepy chiseled faces looking skyward. It's a perfect square, from what I can tell, and all the ornamentation makes it oddly difficult to find the doors from the street.

There's no one in the front office, but I can hear the sound of voices and I follow them down the dim hall. The stone walls are emblazoned with tarnishing plaques. GIRLS' TENNIS STATE CHAMPIONSHIP 1994. GIRLS' LACROSSE REGIONAL FINALISTS 1979. Dust shimmers in each of the window casements. Every room in the hallway is dark, except one, midway down, and so I slow my steps as I reach it. Someone has propped its door open with a book—a black-bound tome with rippled pages. The crack in the doorframe acts like a vent, drawing the subterranean air down along the hallway, sucking it into the classroom around the obstruction of my body like a draught racing into the depths of a well.

From my vantage point at the corner of the room, I can see everything. In the far end there are students at easels, flicking pastels across the clothespinned papers in front of them as if they are pantomiming, underscoring each gesture with a dab of green or red, then rubbing the remnants of it away. In the middle of the room, three students bend over a map—its corners are held to the tabletop by gray geodes. Everything in the room is undulating with the moving air from a fan—anything light enough to blow away must be secured, or it could take wing through the open window and be gone.

And in the front, a teacher at the blackboard—she is tapping the chalk against the cloudy slate for emphasis—an equation, the line of a verse—*Learn this*; *Know this*—and the girl standing next to her clasps the twisted rope of her brown hair to her chest and nods dutifully. All unremarkable interactions, but standing there, I see not one of these children is Leah.

There are plenty of reasonable explanations for my daughter's absence—a trip to the drinking fountain, a quick foray to the school library for a book, or to the supply closet for a particular crayon in a desired shade of blue. I do not know why my mind always jumps to the worst thing. Leah has always dawdled in any secluded nook she can find—underneath the porch where she'd been sent to retrieve a ball, in the restrooms at gas stations—running her fingers across the dirty mirrors or gazing up at the dusty chinks of light, the sky tangled in our trellis. *Leah, Leah,* we would call her. Paul would snap his fingers in the air. And she would jump and come back to us, but there was always a lag in her gaze that betrayed a reluctance she could not disguise.

I do not waste any more time waiting for a rational explanation to present itself. I push open the door and step into the room. A few of the students glance up at me. One boy expectantly pushes up the glasses on his nose.

"Can I help you?" asks the woman at the blackboard. She is dressed like Sister Clarence, the same blouse and blue skirt, her auburn hair combed back from her face, but, unlike Sister Clarence, she is not plain. Her austerity makes her beautiful; its hard lines accentuate the flawless clarity of her every feature and the porcelain glow beneath their golden freckling. There's a quality about her that is almost otherworldly, a radiant sureness that manifests itself in all her brisk gestures. When she wipes her hands on her skirt, chalky afterimages blur across the navy fabric, like the whiteness of her fingers coming away.

When I tell her I am Leah's mother, that I am coming to claim her, she shakes her head at me. "Leah is out today. She wasn't in by nine, so we marked her absent. It's a voluntary program, as you know, so we don't call to verify. Illness—we assumed—or—you didn't know?"

Everyone is staring now. The kids with the map have lost the thread of whatever border they were tracing; still hunched over the table, the trio eyes me with consternation. "If I knew that, would I be here now?"

"I'm sorry, Mrs. Fletcher." Her hand hesitates in the space between us, dithering at my elbow. "There's probably just been some kind of miscommunication. If you'll—"

Out on the street, a motorcycle hurtles past, its open throttle crescendoing to an almost unbearable pinnacle of sound. The children fling their hands to their ears; the end of her sentence is gone. *See, I was right. I was right all along*, is what I want to say—although this solicitous young woman with her touch of parochial beauty would have no idea what I was talking about. To Paul. Paul, if he were here, instead of hours behind us, coming to in a twilit dawn, watching a pattern of terns veer across the sky, up in those remote latitudes. *See, Paul, I was right all along*. It would be arduous to prove that point, arranging all those words, marshaling them through the phone line. I wouldn't even know where to begin.

"Mrs. Fletcher." My tinny name in the silence still ringing with all the clamor of sound. But I'm already turning, pulling the door toward me, and letting it fall heavily closed between us.

What should I do? Where should I go? Where would she have gone, if not here? What could have waylaid her, my daughter, burdened with more filial duty than any one child should rightfully possess? Vivid disasters rise up before me; strange crumbling side streets I have never walked engulf her in their shadows. *The amazing thing*, Paul told me once, *is not that tragedy befalls people, but that it doesn't*. That was years ago, when he'd come back from Sarajevo, during the war. I'd seen only one picture from that trip—a bicycle fallen to the pavement after the teenage boy riding it had caught the bullet of a sniper. The aesthetics of the image were so graceful, you couldn't quite believe it hadn't been arranged—the crumpled chain unfurling, curving droplets darkening the pavement like the dappled shadows of something just taken flight. The boy died in an ambulance on the way to the hospital. I did not ask Paul how he had come by this information nor how he'd had the presence of mind to lean over and make that beautiful photograph in the middle of all that chaos. It was the last time I could remember him saying something like that to me about his work. For months after that he hadn't slept well. Night after night, I'd wake up and the bed next to me would be empty, although I never felt him leaving.

The air is scouring now, carrying grains of dust as stinging as sand, as if they have been blown here from the ocean, miles away. A couple struggles past hand in hand, their T-shirts hiked up over their noses to protect them from the flying debris. And right then, tucked in a pocket flat against my thigh, I find it—the torn piece of paper I picked up two nights ago from the baseboard—a scrap I have been carrying with me, unknowing, all these hours, that bears Leah's script, two words: *O brightness.* The inscription only coming clear to me now. The opening of a Cummings sonnet or maybe part of a litany she was expected to learn by heart. Its plaintive ballpoint loops, each dead-end serif, sharp and thin across the paper's dingy creases.

Under an overpass, over a bridge, right on one block, left

on another. After days of empty quiet, the streets suddenly seem full of passersby on foot, all hurrying past me with purpose, hunched, their shirts and bags ballooning with the raging air. I am the only one with my head up in the smarting gusts, the only one searching every face. I keep catching glimpses—a tender white part, a fragile and determined jawline, a knock-kneed gait, a bookbag strap dangling carelessly from a hand—and I have to catch my breath. But each of these transforms into something else as it comes closer, mirages in the flickering gray afternoon.

Past a dark school, its facade bearing mismatched bricks, some red, some crusted barnacle gray. A troupe of girls standing out on the steps in front, dancing, each motion beautifully in sync: the brisk one-two clap, the collective leap, collective landing, hips grinding in a single defiant provocation. Past a desolately empty swimming pool, wildflowers growing from its depths. Leaves, stripped from their branches, churn through the air as though we are being hurtled through summer into fall. Every detail in the flickering world sears itself upon me, rife with meaning, like things I have already lost. Past a church, a starry window shining in a lone white spire.

Back through the park. Trash whirls over the grass in funnels that merge and separate again. In the fountain, the sky shears apart into droplets. The homeless woman has returned to her bench. She sits impassively, watching the hem of her skirt flail as if it's alive. As I approach, she lifts her head and stares toward me. But it isn't me she's looking at after all. I see that as soon as I glance back and up. It's a streetlight, which has come on above our heads, mistimed, or maybe sensing the dark, the way they somehow do. Behind me, lights are glittering, first one narrow wedge of the city and then another, farther to the east. They are switching on the neighborhoods cautiously, one at a time.

"The stars," the woman mutters. "They've turned them back on. I'd thought they'd never get around to it." Then she reaches out, absently pats the air by my knee, sighs, and turns away again back into herself.

It's how nerves would sound if they came back to life with an utterance. All along the streets the wires singing and thrumming with energy after the days of quiet, electrons hissing along the lines, insulators giving off blue auras against the darkening sky. For some reason people are coming out of their houses to look, hands tipped above their squinted eyes—like it's some kind of miracle, something taken away from us just as inexplicably being given back.

But the house is still dark. I see it as soon as I turn onto the street. Our townhouse sits at the very end of the row—the windowpanes in all the dwellings between shine in tints of varying brightness, but mine are varnished an empty gray. At the sight of them, I falter at last, bending down like a runner caving in at the finish line. It's been harder than I realized, walking those miles in the wind. I left my watch on the basin at the hospital; I have lost all track of time. Surely there must have been lights on the night the power went out—the lamp Leah was reading by. Even over the wind, I can hear Ansel howling, a lugubrious and throaty elegy that

Leah once said made her think of dinosaurs. He used to always howl during storms when the barometric pressure plunged, and the tree branches careened across the roof, giving vent, I believed, to some primordial anxiety that could not be allayed. But he hasn't done it in a long time, too deaf to hear storms or anything else.

Above Leah's pointed little garret, something stirs. A black shape coalescing. There she is, standing on the roof, poised on the edge, looking up and out into the sky, watching the light come and go. Leah. Her arms are outstretched, fingers straining the air. She is right at the very peak, her bare toes lined up along the overburdened gutter, leaning forward as if to test whether or not the open space will bear her weight. Her face is contemplative, lips parted, forehead furrowed in what I must accept is her resting expression. She will age quickly, my daughter—that small and persistent hieroglyph etched between her eyes deepening and spreading, taking on new lines, and the thought of them is terrible to me. A photograph of her taken at this moment might render a sense of the heights in which she stands, the way the world's three dimensions seem distilled into two, light and dark shapes locked together, the fragile lacework of her fingers twined in the ethereal air, the thinness of the apex on which she is balanced. But I do not believe it would convey the fierce resoluteness of her stance or the sense that she is not a person who will be consoled. That is what I think. But then she looks down at me, the light of the sky shining in her eyes, exalted and transforming. And I can't help it—I hold out my arms, welcoming her back to earth.

152

BLIGHT

KATHERINE WENT BLIND THE spring the trees started dying.

A profusion of storms that season—the kind that burst across the sky like sprinters from the starting block and die just as quickly—forced her husband, Peter, away from his desk and out into the world with the men who worked for him. He became nothing more than a pair of hands wielding a chainsaw, carving his way through the wreckage left by the wind.

On his third job of the year, the final Sunday of April, he drove the truck. When he turned the corner and saw the house down at the end of the little cul-de-sac Peter lifted his foot off the gas and coasted along, staring in amazement. The boy in the passenger seat next to him whistled quietly.

Limbs in violent disarray lay strewn across the grass, the driveway, the street, the roof. Branches had clawed their way along the yellow paint trailing thin seismographic scratches behind them and gnarled up the second-story gutters. Splinters bristled from every windowsill. It wasn't that the trees had snapped away at the top; the gusts from the previous night had torn them from the earth at the roots. The sod gaped with holes; the lawn, no longer a planed green surface, folded over on itself in crests and troughs, treacherous footing that swelled away on either side. The marbled clods still gleamed wet and raw from their evisceration. Peter climbed out and stood mulling over the scene before him. The winds could have been stronger here, he thought, but even so . . . Those maples were young. Their flowing sap should have limbered them up and allowed them to cling to the soil better than that. He propped his elbow on the truck's side mirror and tried to assemble a plausible scenario in his head.

Mrs. Potter, wearing only a flapping blue bathrobe, flung open the door and raced down the first few stairs toward him until a trunk lying across the herringbone path brought her up short. She could not climb over it and hold the robe closed at the same time, and she was reluctant to attempt the scramble in front of these strange men. So she shielded her eyes and stared in Peter's direction.

"Thank God you came so quickly," she called out to him. "As you can see, we can't even get out of the house." She squinted skyward. "We didn't know what hit us. We got up this morning, and there was so much *light*." An image of instantaneous disintegration flashed before her eyes, but she couldn't place its origin. "We're going to turn into stone . . . or dust. What is it I'm thinking of?"

He shrugged and wondered if he should tell her that in the fifteen years since he took over the business this was one of the worst messes he had ever seen. It might impress her.

She smiled at his reticent gesture. "Never mind," she said. "We're about to sell the house soon. This could make it easier. We'll pay whatever it is you charge. Just take away the shambles." And with that, she turned back and made her way inside, her bare feet slapping softly on the stones.

Matt rummaged in the bed of the truck, hauling out the saws, and began to fill them with gas while Peter called down his list of backup employees. Only Vince and Chris answered their phones. They would be at this all day.

They set upon the largest tree—a white pine, dying needles already stiffening and losing their pelt-like softness— dismantling it into pieces they could haul back to the truck. After they finished Peter sent Matt, the youngest and most agile of the four of them, to clear off the roof while he and Vince took apart the maple that spread across the driveway.

Before they began, Peter, chainsaw in one hand, stretched his back and straightened up to watch Matt's silhouette flash against the sun, now balanced on the peak of a dormer. He revved the saw, let it fall carelessly against the trunk at his knee. The teeth bit in at first, then sank down through the unresisting wood.

The unexpected speed of the saw's descent threw him off-balance. Peter nearly fell face-first. When he pulled out the blade and looked into the new fissure in the tree trunk, Peter saw something he had never seen before. He wasn't sure his eyes weren't tricking him; he'd spent all morning in the glaring light having forgotten his sunglasses. But no. After he made a few more incisions along the length of the trunk, he pulled out a few cross-sections and took a long look.

Red, like rust or dried blood, coated the inside of the tree. When Peter peeled off his gloves and brushed the velvety surface, feathery spores clung to his fingertips. The guts of the trunk were gone, eaten away completely—all those rings, the traces of that hidden and singular history. An irregular hollow space ran up the center like a drained artery. When Peter stuck his head down and peered into it he could see daylight filtering through the tangles of the roots.

He examined his smeared fingers again, held them up to his nose, and breathed in the strangely sweet smell they emanated. A fungus, he thought, or the by-product of some bacteria, but he had never witnessed anything like it. Whatever it was, it had devoured the tree with incredible speed from the inside out. The budding of the maple had been only slightly retarded. Not until he checked closer as he was doing now did he observe it, maybe two weeks behind what you would expect this time of year.

They found it in four more trees, including a birch on the perimeter of the yard. From there, an uninhabited patch of woods stretched into the distance for about a mile until the next subdivision, and Peter stood staring into its depths for a long moment before he turned back to work.

When the men threw the piles into the chipper, bloody silt wafted up in the still air. Peter took one of the cross-sections and tossed it into the back of the truck just before they left for the evening. The Potters, long since departed for a dinner function, had left the check on the dining room table for him, and Peter washed his hands in their powder room before he picked it up and tucked it carefully into his wallet.

After he finished cleaning out the trucks and parking them in the back lot, Peter made a call to Jerome, a friend who worked in the Forestry Department down at Michigan State. The office voice mail said he'd be in by the end of the week. Peter wrapped the dingy phone cord around and around his index finger and stared through the office window into the gray spring twilight as he listened to Jerome's recorded voice. The chime sounded and he said, "Jerome, it's Peter. I have something here—I don't know if you've seen it, but if you haven't, you'll definitely want to take a look." Then he hung up and went home.

By the time Peter walked through the front door, Katherine was in bed but not sleeping. The amber lamplight blurred the outline of his figure. He did not drop down next to her as he usually did, leaves in his hair, boots still laced to his feet. He said he wanted to shower first, then disappeared into the bathroom shucking clothes as he went.

He stayed under the spray longer than usual; she'd finished an entire chapter before he shut the water off. She would need to start over again when he emerged, the odor of sap clinging to him as it always did, only slightly diluted by the soap and shampoo. When at last he lay down and rolled over to kiss her once on each eyelid, Katherine reached for the last folded-down page, smoothed it open, and read aloud: "When the young Dawn with finger tips of rose made heaven bright . . ."

She was obliging him tonight, Peter thought, reading Homer. He hadn't picked up a book in years, not since he'd dropped out of college his sophomore year. It was the books that drove him away, so many of them—he couldn't stand it. All that print on the page, like a line of black knots, tangled him up. He made it to a paragraph's end and could not remember the beginning.

None of those words meant anything at all to him until Katherine's voice gave them their cadence. He knew he imposed his preferences upon her during their nightly readings—asking her for Hemingway, Steinbeck, Carver, and Kent Haruf, then making no effort to stay awake when she spread open the pages of Lawrence or Hawthorne. She'd attempted to read him Gertrude Stein once; he pulled the covers over his head begging her to make it stop. She found it funny—a man who didn't read professing such strong literary tastes.

The Greek classics were among his particular favorites. Peter liked to envision the warriors as men of immense stature, their bodies tough as oaks. He saw the trajectory of blades through the air, swords swinging, biting into, and carving flesh as unyielding as hardwood—felling those soldiers would be as arduous as demolishing trees. The earth, he imagined, would tremble when they were brought low.

Peter closed his eyes, and the words lapped into his ears one after another until sleep blurred then extinguished them entirely.

Halfway into a stanza, Katherine lost the line on the page. It disappeared as if into a sunspot, a blazing white corona with a dark preposition on either side. She blinked twice, then a third time before it came back into focus. But still a single dark spot hung just in the corner of her peripheral vision. Peter had fallen asleep; the hiccup in her reading did not stir him. She closed the book and laid it on the nightstand. She thought, So it's finally time. She'd had excellent vision her entire life, but she was forty-two now, and she knew sooner or later the decline of her body would intrude. She'd heard the complaints of her friends. An old receipt lay next to the lamp. She picked up a pencil and across the back of it wrote the words *eye doctor*. Then she turned out the light.

When she called the next day to make an appointment, the receptionist said the doctor would see her at the end of the week, in the afternoon, a half hour after school let out. The fact that the woman emitted a long *hmm* when Katherine described her symptoms should have alerted her, but it did not.

In the doctor's chair a series of silver circles were dropped and lifted before her gaze. The pale green walls, with their unsettling posters of the human eyeball as some sort of vein-riddled grub, ballooned and dwindled in front of her. She couldn't quite sit comfortably. The doctor seemed less interested in letting her pore over the charts than he did in shining a light in her eyes and looking again and again.

When he was certain, he sat down on the stool next to her chair and told her that she had a rare form of retinitis pigmentosa. It was a degenerative disease of the eyes. Her vision would deteriorate over a period of weeks, he said, maybe months, until she lost her sight entirely. There were a few ophthalmologists out east working on some procedures, but the success rate was exceedingly poor, and so the disease was still considered irreversible.

At the word *irreversible* he lost her. She looked hard into the man's face. His irises were the color of steel, but she didn't think of that word exactly. The impression simply registered somewhere dimly within her and sank to the bottom. She could not understand him at all and realized, with a shock, the question in his mind (if indeed there was one at all) was the precise inverse of her own. *Why* not *you?* his dry gaze asked her. The problem had been solved; his intellect was no longer required. Looking at a completed puzzle was never enjoyable. The diversion lay in fitting the pieces together, and that was finished now.

Only when she stood up from the chair, fumbled for her purse, and spilled a collection of cylinders across the bristly carpet—lipstick, mascara, tampons, pencils—did the doctor feel moved. He stooped to help her gather her belongings (but not the tampons) and tuck them away again. He asked in a gruff voice if his receptionist might call someone for her, but she shook her head and clutched her checkbook resolutely to her chest as she edged her way to the door.

As she walked home through the sunlight, the cold breeze soaking like a liquid through the thin layer of her sweater, across town, Jerome returned her husband's phone call. When Peter answered Jerome did not say hello. Instead he said, "What is this I am hearing about the trees?"

Katherine staggered down a drainage ditch next to the baseball diamond, grabbed a fencepost with both hands, let the strut dig like a fist into her stomach and tried to breathe while two boys flashing past on bicycles slowed down to marvel at the sight of the woman impaled on the fence, gasping for air.

Peter came home late again. When she heard him open the door and the creak of his steps crossing the threshold Katherine thought, at last, here was someone who would understand the profoundness of this day's passing. She lay quietly, chest weighted down, and waited for him to push the bedroom door open.

The house was dark; the burners on the stove were bare and cool. He found her in bed, the Bible of all things, open to Ecclesiastes, resting across her breasts. He eyed the translucent pages with their text cleaved into two columns, and his heart sank with sudden misgiving.

She was so composed when she told him; the hours had given her such a head start that she was leagues ahead, taken out by a current that rushed her away, trailing her fingers as she went, dabbling them in the degrees of loss, feeling its myriad fluctuations, the great and the small. Already she grappled with consequences he could not yet comprehend. He thought he would never catch up.

They lay there on the bed together while the last of the red light died out from behind the shrouded windowpane. When he finally leaned over to kiss her eyelids, the right then the left, he lingered on each trembling sheath of skin, parting his lips, tasting the salt in the creases and damp lashes, softly exhaling his useless breath over them.

And yet, somehow, the trees still had to be considered. The next morning Jerome drove an hour north from East Lansing. His pickup rattled along the straight niche of highway that parted the expansive fields on either side into a flicker of dark and clotted furrows. The flat land of central Michigan stretched out before him and a mottled ceiling of altostratus clouds hung just overhead. It was if he were passing through a dwindling crevice amid the glacial merging of two immense planes. And mile after mile flowing past bristled with the first leaves thrusting out that bright green shock, lurid in the gray air.

His first stop in town was Peter's office. When Peter presented the cross-section, Jerome turned the circle around and around in his hands. The center was so rotten that the wooden disk nearly crumbled into shards. The days in the ventilated office air had diminished its reddish cast. It could be a hundred different things, Jerome knew. He slid it into a plastic bag marked for Diagnostic Services.

After that they went out looking. The Potters were not at home. The windowpanes were dim; a realtor's lockbox hung on the door, and a new For Sale sign stood in the yard. The disheveled earth had been smoothed back down into place, its brown traces rinsed away by the rain.

There was no one to grant or deny them permission, so they passed without hesitation through the open space of the lawn and plunged into the thicket behind the house. Almost instantly the neighborhood vanished behind them. Neither man said a word as their footsteps carried them across the forest floor. The pack on Jerome's back beat out a quiet accompanying rhythm to their strides.

Jerome's profession had taken him into forests all over the American continents from the Yukon to Brazil and the years spent trekking through these varying ecosystems had honed each of his senses. Or maybe it was not so much each one in particular but their integration. Now, in this diminutive patch of wooded land, he thought something was not right. But he couldn't pinpoint the dissonance, whether it might be the stillness, the dimness of the first green buds, or the peculiar odor in the air. Forewarning had a way of priming false alarms. During dry seasons he often scented wildfires that did not exist. But he smelled something now, a strange cloying stench, a whiff of rot that made him think, reluctantly, of gangrene.

Just two steps ahead of him, Peter lifted his eyes from the imbricated pattern of last year's leaves beneath his feet and stopped short. Jerome rocked back on his heels, nearly went down. *There*, Peter said and pointed through the gloom.

Before them a stand of birches lay fallen together in a pile, twenty trees, maybe more. It was impossible to ascertain the exact number from where they stood. The periphery of the ghostly pale jumble disappeared into the darkness beyond the clearing.

It was as if, Peter thought, a man had gone at these trees with a buzz saw, whirling his way through the cluster of them, bringing down everything he touched. No, that description was not right—this was something else entirely. There were no silted trails of shavings, no splintered bark, no shorn stumps, no raw odor of sap left hanging in the air. Here each tree lay unscathed, silver drops beaded along each smooth white limb that glowed against the rain-soaked ground.

Hastily, Peter reached to brush the flecks of dew from the shoulders of his jacket and the cuffs of his sleeves in an attempt to keep off the chill. But he shivered anyway.

Up ahead, Jerome thrashed through the foliage, feeling around, gaping. "Look." He held up his smeared and rusty hands. Then he bent down and vanished again, but his muttering remained audible like the repetitive call of a nearby bird: "What the hell, What the hell."

For two hours the men plundered the carnage while overhead the clouds thickened, and a perpendicular rain penetrated the forest canopy and soaked them drop by drop. The momentum belonged mostly to Jerome. He tore away leaves, lopped off branches, took swabs, and bored into the trunks of surrounding trees. He made one call after another; the reception in the clearing was all but nonexistent. He shouted into the phone about pathogens and cross-species contamination. The presence of this death, strange and inexplicable, made him avid in a way that set Peter ill at ease. "No," Jerome said. "Do you understand? It's not just the birches. I'm finding it in everything. The maples—Hello? Hello? Dammit!" And he threw the phone into the bushes.

What could Peter say to Katherine? What did she care about trees when the world was dropping away piece by piece? A week after her appointment, she foresaw how it all would unfold—the most tedious kind of narrative. The darkening spots would multiply and spread across her field of vision like moths eating away at everything she saw. First like watching birds against the sun. Then like peering through a trellis. Then looking through a night sky, only pinpoints of remaining light beaming their way through. Then nothing.

The house she and Peter owned was only a mile from the high school, so Katherine walked to work in the mornings and home in the afternoons. Through autumn and winter and spring, her peregrinations took her through a baseball diamond, a soccer field, past tennis courts, and a stone fountain that ran and went dry with the seasons, turned on and off again by an unknown hand.

One morning, walking through the park, three dark spots hovering like harpies in her peripheral vision, Katherine looked up and saw the branches of an ash tree. A single yellow limb touched by premature fall or an unknown defect hung from the green leaves above it like a golden chandelier.

Like a golden chandelier. That phrase repeated itself over and over, like a refrain to her walking, the rest of the way to school and then through her first period class on American literature.

When the bell rang she picked up a composition note-book left over from the pile she distributed to her students and opened it. On the fading first line she wrote the words down in black ink and then looked at them for a long moment. When she finally lifted her eyes, then closed them, then looked down again, it was still there, the image preserved and clear. For the first time in two weeks, since the moment she sat in that doctor's chair, she felt a faint sensation of relief, no more than a breath, but it was some-thing. She set the notebook down and gazed out the window to where a few intrepid birds plucked at the softening ground.

After the final class of the day, she tucked the notebook under her elbow and walked home. As she crossed through the parking lot, she chanted the line of a poem they'd been discussing. "Because I could not stop for Death—He kindly stopped for me . . ." But when she stepped off the pavement onto the grass, the words of the Amherst poet died from her mind. She stared up into the sky overhead, studied two clouds splitting away like cells dividing, and between them . . . Somewhere in her bag there was a pen; she fumbled for it among the detritus in the cloth depths. When she found it she pulled it out and on the second line of the note-book's first page she wrote: *a cleft of blue sky.*

Without thinking she placed the pen between her teeth

and left it there as she continued on. By the tennis courts, she stopped again. *The hurricane fence parsing the sunlight into diamond-shaped beams.* The rest of the way home she traversed in fits and starts, turning her head in every direction, taking it all in. And then, just before she turned from the sidewalk onto her driveway, another spot, a new one. That made four.

The next day, while Peter sat at the desk in the office laboring his way through columns of numbers, punching them into an obsolete computer that dimmed and brightened with each computation, a man from the DNR strode through the front entrance. He was there, he said, to offer Peter a contractor position. The state wanted to utilize all available local resources in the removal of the diseased trees. And they would need to move as quickly as possible.

Peter shook his head: no thanks. He said he had no desire to be in the employ of the government, not even temporarily. And although he did not say it out loud, he knew he did not want to work with a man who used the word *utilize*. He shrugged his shoulders. "Sorry," he said, "but I really just do small jobs, construction clearing, salvage, that type of work."

The DNR man scratched his nose patiently and gave a little smile as he gazed around and took in the dingy walls with their wood paneling, the water-stained corner in the back next to the bathroom. "Of course it's your decision," he said, "but if we don't get this thing contained soon, there's not going to be much to salvage. It'll be pretty bad for business." He handed Peter his card. "We could use your help. Think about it."

As if Peter did anything these days but think. At night if Katherine did not turn on the overhead lights, she struck her hip on chairs, on tables, on doorframes. She stumbled over the words on the page. Peter watched these falterings, and his thoughts whirred on, taking him into darker and darker recesses. The disjointed syllables made him think how much hangs on a pair of consonants or a single vowel—inky folds holding within them an ocean's space of meaning— the separation of *stars* from *stairs*, *breathing* from *beating*, *looking* from *losing*. From somewhere next to him and far away he heard Katherine's voice imbued with a brittle new inflection: "That's all, Peter. Good night." And the lamp blinked out.

When he came home the next evening he found her in the kitchen, holding up a slice of tomato to the window, staring through the translucent red wedge while the pink juice trickled down around her wrist. A pen nestled in the nook behind her left ear.

He thought maybe something had happened. "What are you doing?" he asked.

Her hand fell to her side; her face flushed. "Nothing," she said, "I was just looking." She closed the notebook—with its black letters on the front that said *COMPOSITION* in all uppercase letters—sitting on the table in front of her. Right then he finally almost said something to her about the trees, the dying, the condescending DNR man. Instead he simply ruffled her pale hair and turned away.

Katherine opened the book again when he left and plucked the cap off her pen. *Seeds glistening with rosy slime.* She went back to making dinner, cutting away at the gritty leeks and sautéing the tiny green circlets until the small kitchen filled with the reek of them.

When Peter called the DNR man to tell him he'd reconsidered, he wasn't in, but his secretary said, "Yes, Peter Clark. Daniel said you'd be calling."

The Department of Natural Resources owned huge trucks, trucks that could hold small bodies of water and saws that could fell elephants or dismember whales. The wheels of their vehicles churned the Potter's yard to mush, but the Potters had moved out by then. And the real estate agent had given up and gone away in despair.

They went to work, tearing the forest apart, bringing it down—any tree with a mottled leaf, a sagging branch, a listing angle, pockmarked bark. The woods raged with the sound of an army of saws and the birds fled. Men trampled saplings with their boots, scattered puddles with their feet, ripped down vines, crushed the ferns, obliterated spiderwebs, and kicked anthills to rubble. They attempted to delineate the path of the disease, to mark the perimeter of the blight. They carried buckets of red paint and marked the trunks of the survivors with a bright dab. *This one lives, this one lives, this one dies.*

It took them three days. Then they burned everything inside that red ring to the ground. Peter did not stay to watch, but miles down the road he looked in the rearview mirror and saw the crematory smoke blackening the sky.

As he drove, he remembered how Katherine, in jest, used to call him a tree undertaker. Coming in after the storms, she said, bearing away the dead. What would she say now, if she knew?

When he got back to the office, there was a message from a man on the west side of town, the other side. He said, "There's something wrong with a couple of my trees. I think they're about to come down."

The high school was too far away from the fire for anyone to see or smell the smoke. While her students clustered in small groups discussing *The Grapes of Wrath*, Katherine counted the spots. There were eleven now, spreading out irregularly like Rorschach designs before her eyes. But she wouldn't conjecture, she wouldn't contrive a story.

When class let out, Katherine wandered up and down the halls with her notebook. *Blackboards dusted with white as if zephyrs had brushed past and left their traces there.* In the math room, *White chalk points make constellations that spread out along the x and y axes.*

On the way home, when she stared down at her feet *a glob of spittle, opalescent on the sidewalk, tiny bubbles still caught inside.* When she looked overhead, *squirrels disappearing like brown smoke plumes into the tree branches.* When she gazed to her right, *children ricocheting like molecules across the playing field.* Her hand ached, she nearly fell over a crack, and the pen tore a line through the paper.

She took a deep breath and tried to slow down, to think of something else. She remembered the Homer she was reading to Peter. She might make it to the end before she was overtaken but maybe not. And he'd been tired these days during their nightly readings, which made her angry. There she was, pressing valiantly onward across the page while he stared blankly through the window into the night at something she couldn't see.

A daughter of Katherine's friend was getting married in Saginaw that weekend, just a small backyard gathering at dusk beneath a tent. They forgot about it until the night before, so Peter had to drive out after work to scavenge the stores for a gift, something presentable. Finally, in an over-priced boutique—the town's only really pretentious store—he settled upon a pair of silver-plated candlesticks, tall, heavy, ornate.

They sat on Katherine's lap during the half-hour drive. M-20, the most direct route, would have taken them through the worst part of the mauled landscape, so he made up an excuse about roadwork and headed north, then east, then south—ten miles out of their way. She did not seem to find anything amiss, and she did not seem to see the stark white signs just beyond the city limits declaring that no lumber or firewood should cross county lines. He accelerated as they passed them, just in case.

She traced her fingernail along the paper creases of the

heavy bundle in her lap and reflected on how an outdoor wedding in the Michigan spring was a gamble. But then so was a marriage. So was opening your eyes in the morning.

The tent was beautiful, a luminous cluster of pyramids in the deepening twilight. The trees waved in the wind throwing their pale pink flowers against the sky. Somewhere in the distance an imminent storm collected itself. Just as the guests were settling into the chairs the rain let down. The women in the wedding party gathered their skirts and raced through the grass with the graceful off-balance strides of women running in heels—always one step from falling. *The graceful off-balance strides.* Katherine wanted to write that line but she had brought a frivolous silver purse—not big enough to hold a wallet—that matched her dress. Her dependable everyday bag with her composition book sat at home next to the coatrack or maybe the dining room table. She didn't even have a pen.

All through the ceremony, she repeated the words over and over to herself, afraid of losing them, but one impression after another—dozens, hundreds—percolated up, and for each one she retained she lost ten others. She could hardly sit still; she was almost weeping. Peter felt her stirring next to him, hunching over, and then straightening in her seat. The guests sitting behind her were afraid she was going to be ill.

As soon as the bride and groom passed back down the aisle, joined together for this world and maybe the next, Katherine pulled Mary aside. "Do you have a pen and some paper?" The look on her face was so strained that at first Mary could not understand what she was asking—she thought it must be something urgent and terribly embarrassing. Then she picked up a napkin off one of the tables, said, "Here, you can write on this."

And Peter, dutifully doling out his congratulations to the groom, looked up when he heard Katherine almost shrieking from across the tented space. "No, no, I need something that will last!" He saw the woman, looking askance, step away from his wife, once so self-possessed, as if she were the ranting lady on the bus, the one always left ringed by a circle of empty seats.

When Mary retrieved a pad of paper and a pencil from the house and brought it to her, Katherine flushed. "I'm sorry. I'm so sorry," she said.

"It's fine." Mary waved her hand lightly in the air. But she wouldn't meet Katherine's eye.

During the dinner and the dancing that followed, Katherine sat on a chair next to the entrance of the tent, where she could see both inside and out—where the storm raged in the distance. Her hand only stopped forming letters long enough to flick to a new page. *Grass seething in the wind, lightning like roots burrowing into the night sky, glints of light swimming like fish in the water glasses, skirts whirling, dancing bodies revolving like planets.*

The music blurred in her ears, meaningless, as if she had plunged her head beneath water, but during a break between songs, a space of sudden and blessed quiet, she heard a man talking to Peter, a conversation she had missed the beginning of.

"The paper is calling it the tree plague," the man said.

Katherine did not know him. "They're saying it could be in Saginaw County in a matter of weeks. Weeks! I know you've been working with the DNR—do they have any idea what kind of toll—"

She dropped the pencil and twisted around to look, really look, at Peter. Their gazes met over his interlocutor's shoulder and past the black holes that hovered there in that interim space between them. They stared at each other for so long that the stranger stopped talking, turned his head, searching for an explanation, the rhythm of his monologue lost.

They were the first couple to leave. Peter carried their jackets on one arm and guided Katherine through the night with the other, back to the car. He was tired. He did not want to drive the long way home. So he turned the car onto M-20, and the highway bore them dead west, a straight line back, no detours, no diversions. The rain spread across their windshield, droplets as fine as dust, but then larger splashes that burst and blew apart in the wind.

The white headlights in the oncoming lane of traffic made Katherine think of a strand of pearls being dragged over a black tabletop, but her fingers were cramped, and it was too dark for her to see the words on the page, so she let the thought dissipate.

Instead, she turned her head and struggled to make out Peter's profile, difficult although it was close and should have been one shape she knew better than anything else. There was no way for her to describe it that she could hold on to. Faces were the trickiest forms to render—harder than light, than substance, than motion. She'd spent an hour last night in front of the mirror trying to capture her own eyes, their surface pattern but also the depths of them. And she'd come away empty-handed. Nothing but a blank page.

As the car drew them to the eastern perimeter of town, Peter saw the wasteland of trees before Katherine, of course. He wasn't sure if she would make it out at all. A jagged and empty space, everything blanketed with wet ash, everything still, even in the wind and rain, covered over with night but not to be revived by morning. A thousand splinters to wound the eye and that muscle that pulsed insistently on in the cavity of his chest.

If only, he thought, it were someone else driving this car into this storm, passing this patch of dark and ravaged land. Maybe it was simply his desire to avoid suffering, but he didn't think so. There are times when you wish your anguish on someone worthier than you, someone able to give the terrible scene its due. Like Hemingway transforming the savagery and gore of a bullfight into something beautiful, or Homer immortalizing the sprawling wastes of battle. When it was his turn to pick up the book, to struggle his way across the page, how would he fare? His breathing faltered; he did not know if he was up for the task ahead, but he kept his hands on the steering wheel and his foot on the accelerator, kept driving them westward into the storm.

And finally the car drew close enough and, staring out the window, she could pick out the tree shards like bones, looming up in the headlights that flashed past, blanched shapes that curled upward through the shining air toward the sky briefly before the darkness extinguished them. She was afraid to look away thinking suddenly it might be the last sight she saw. So she didn't turn her head when, beside her, he pronounced her name. "Katherine." She only said, "Yes. Yes. I see it too."

ACKNOWLEDGMENTS

Thank you. Thank you as always to my wonderful agent, Rayhané Sanders, for all your hard work and diligent reminders. Thank you to my kind editor, Rachel Mannheimer, and to Gleni Bartels and to the rest of the team at Bloomsbury.

I wrote these stories while I was in the M.F.A. program at George Mason University. Thank you to everyone there who read them and shared their thoughts and encouragement: my friends, my writing group cohorts, and my professors Susan Shreve, Courtney Brkic, and Steve Goodwin. An especially heartfelt thanks to the inimitable Alan Cheuse. When I manage to squeeze in the time to write these days, it is your voice I hear, urging me on against the odds.

Most of all: thank you to my family who pulled together during the difficult past year, who occasionally took the helm when I needed to steal away from the hospital and get some editing done. Thank you, Mom and Dad. Thank you, Martha Albrecht. Thank you, Michael. I couldn't have done it without you.

ABOUT THE AUTHOR

Alyson Foster is the author of the novel *God is an Astronaut*. She earned her B.A. in creative writing from the University of Michigan, winning a Hopwood Award for her fiction, and received her M.F.A. from George Mason University, where she was a Completion Fellow. Her short fiction has appeared in publications including *Glimmer Train*, the *Iowa Review*, *Ascent*, and the *Kenyon Review*. She lives in Washington, D.C.